GW00727882

Ulric: A Dragon's Tale

Ulric: A Dragon's Tale

Jackie McBride

MISTICO
BOOKS

A catalogue record for this book
is available from the British Library

ISBN 0-9553772-0-X
ISBN 978-0-9553772-0-4

Illustrations by Vincent Butler R.S.A. R.G.I.

Printed in the UK

First published in the UK in 2006 by

MISTICO BOOKS
Border Cottage
30 Pine View Close
Haslemere, Surrey
GU27 1DU

www.dragonacres.com

For Barbara and John, Max and Toby – with love

Acknowledgements

My darling husband, Richard, for endlessly discussing my ideas.

Felicity Howard for her suggested editing and valuable encouragement.

Present and past members of The Word Association, especially, Justine, Alexandra, Sarah, Pat and Carol, for their energy, sense of fun and support.

Lynne & Lawrence and Claudia for reading the early drafts.

And to special friends who have been there for me - Connie, Anne, Linda H, Linda M and not forgetting Nana Lou.

To Vincent Butler for capturing Ulric's spirit in the wonderful drawings.

And to Ben Mobbs, who, a long time ago became Ulric's number one fan.

Introduction by Ulric

This is the first in a series of stories about me. I am an old, friendly dragon called Ulric. In this book you'll meet my best friend, a Peregrine Falcon, and some of my favourite relatives.

The tale you are about to read is true. It all happened recently.

Has my biographer, who I call J, shown me in a good light? I think so. Reading about myself I see a dashing, daring, wise dragon, with a kind heart. OK, I can be a little bit grumpy and stubborn, but that's an age thing. (I was born centuries ago.)

However, as you will see I have lots of fun. If you are reading this at bedtime, or someone you love is reading this to you, neither of you will have bad dreams.

This is a happy book. I am a happy dragon.

I hope you enjoy my adventures.

With a warm scaly hug,   Ulric

One

Trick or Treat

Ulric stirred and licked his front claws. Coils of hot breath escaped from his tongue and melted into the October night. Jumping up and down he broke several slabs of marble. Kicking them to one side, he repositioned his ancient body across a bed of assorted rocks and tried to get comfortable. Staring into the night sky he watched a firework explode in the distance.

Above him a Peregrine Falcon watched it too.

On the outskirts of Appleton, in Cedar Crescent, lived the Bristow family. Maggie was in the kitchen scraping seeds from a large pumpkin.

'Make a really scary face,' cried Sophie, and she pointed to a drawing in her Halloween picture book.

'Not too scary,' teased her mother, 'we don't want to frighten Daddy.'

'We do,' yelled Sophie, 'we can put it in the window to scare him when he comes home.'

Maggie smiled. 'It's not Halloween until tomorrow. Oh my goodness, we've forgotten Betsy.'

'Betsy, Betsy,' shouted Sophie, chasing after her mother.

'Poor Betsy,' cooed Maggie, as she lifted a white rabbit from its hutch. 'You hate this time of the year don't you?' she asked, smoothing down Betsy's long ears as she carried her into the warm house.

Contrary to what they thought, Betsy loved this time of the year. Her hutch was brought into the scullery and most evenings she was allowed to run around the sitting room.

'When I'm older,' Sophie told her rabbit, 'I will go trick and treating.'

'Will you now?' said Maggie, who had begun to carve triangular eye sockets into a faceless pumpkin.

At bedtime Sophie insisted that the scary pumpkin was covered with a towel because it was frightening Betsy. She asked her Daddy to read a story from her favourite book. A book about an old dragon.

'I love all dragons,' she said jumping into her little bed and pulling the friendly dragon patterned duvet up to her chin.

'I'm hungry again,' roared Ulric. The Falcon stared

at him without blinking. Ulric was getting old. His bronze scales had lost their lustre and he often looked weary, thought the Falcon, as he flew from their cave. Returning in a trice with a tasty supper dish, he placed it in front of Ulric's long snout.

'Bless you my friend,' said Ulric, 'What would I do without you.' It wasn't said as a question but the Falcon surprised him with an answer.

'You'd survive,' responded the Falcon.

Ulric continued with his feast. He enjoyed having the Falcon as his companion, even though he hardly spoke. Ulric, like most dragons, could read the emotions of other creatures so he always knew what his friend was feeling. In fact that is how the two had first met. Many years ago, Ulric had been flying across the vast expanse of Northumbria when he sensed a creature in distress. Smelling fire he went to investigate. Trapped inside a cage, next to blazing bales of straw was a young male Falcon. Ignoring the crackling fire, Ulric flew to the cage and used his strength to prise apart the metal bars. The frightened Falcon hopped onto the spade of his tail. From that day, the two of them had stayed together.

'This is delicious,' said Ulric, licking his lips. Food provided instant energy and soon he was ready for his evening outing.

Ulric didn't fly great distances anymore. The muscles in his chest, those that supported his wings, had grown weak. His short, thick legs, however, remained sturdy, so he'd take an evening stroll around the quarry, and sometimes venture into the nearby woods and fields.

'Go my friend and check the coast is clear,' shouted Ulric. The Falcon liked being given this signal, sweeping back his wings he was immediately airborne.

The following day, Halloween, was cool and windy. Gold and red leaves danced and cart-wheeled along the country lanes. Some leaves found their way into Ulric's cave. Ulric was sleeping. He'd managed to tuck himself under rocks and slabs of marble, only his head and the spade of his tail were visible.

Back at Cedar Crescent Sophie had been longing to light their pumpkin. As evening approached she sat on the floor with Betsy. Pointing at the pumpkin she spoke quietly into one of Betsy's ears.

'Don't be frightened. It's not real. Not real like dragons are,' she told her rabbit.

That evening it was darker than anyone imagined it

could be. A power cut at 6pm had plunged the town of Appleton into darkness. Maggie lit as many candles as she could find, including the pumpkin. It glowed eerily from the window sill.

'Are you frightened mummy?' asked Sophie. 'Betsy and I are!' she shivered.

A bright crescent moon hung in the night sky.

Remembering it was Halloween, Ulric began to get excited.

'We could take a longer stroll tonight,' he shouted to the Falcon. 'We could go through the town, dance in the street. It is so dark no one will see us.'

The Falcon stared at him without blinking.

'Don't look at me like that, I'd love to go out and party. It is Halloween.'

'Promise to behave yourself then,' said the Falcon.

'What are promises?' asked the dragon, mischievously.

After finishing the feast of field mice, the two of them set off. The Falcon flew ahead and turned from time to time to beckon with his wing. Ulric was no slouch, he ambled through the wood with the energy of a much younger dragon. When they got to the outskirts of Appleton they both stopped.

Ulric sniffed the air and the Falcon knew that he was determined to go further.

'I sense there's a fair little creature somewhere over there who loves me,' said Ulric, pointing with the spade of his tail. 'I must go and find her.'

'It's very dangerous walking on the track,' said the Falcon

'But you mustn't,' cried the Falcon.

'Why not?' asked Ulric.

'You could meet others with less love in their hearts,' warned the Falcon.

It was too late for words of caution. Ulric was running now, charging along, knocking over small trees and trampling on anything that got in his way. Soon he reached a steep bank and without hesitating slid down the side. Landing close to the railway track he looked around. He knew that trains came along here, knew he'd have to listen out for the hurried hurdeler-der, hurdeler-der sound. He looked behind him, then leapt onto the track and ambled along.

'How far are you going?' asked the Falcon, who was flying overhead.

'As far as my instinct takes me,' replied Ulric, striding out.

When they arrived at a fork in the track, Ulric took a deep breath. Choosing to head in the direction that led towards some cottages, he continued. Soon his moon-shadow made strange shapes across the cottage gardens. Soon, thought the Falcon, we'll be at Appleton Station.

'When will Daddy be home?' asked Sophie, pressing her nose against the window.

Maggie held a candle up to the kitchen clock, 'Is that the time?' she asked .

'Daddy knows it's Halloween, he said we could all go out for a walk,' sighed Sophie.

'We will go out for a walk, poppet, but this power cut may delay him.'

'Do trains have power cuts?' asked Sophie.

At that moment Maggie's mobile rang. 'Darling, we were just talking about you,' said Maggie.

'The train has stopped,' said David, 'we're not far from the station.'

'Stopped?' repeated Maggie.

'Yes. The guard tells us they are checking the line. Something large has been seen ahead of us.'

'David, it is Halloween,' laughed Maggie.

'Well, someone reported a dragon-like shape running along the line.'

'A what?' asked Maggie.

'A dragon! I know. I had hoped to be home by now,' sighed David.

'We'll come and meet you. Sophie is longing to go out and the electricity went off an hour ago.'

'What did Daddy say?' asked Sophie.

'His train has been delayed, but he's on his way,' replied Maggie, reaching for the torch and blowing out the candles. 'Go and get your coat, scarf and gloves, I said we'd go and meet him at the station.'

'Yippee!' shouted Sophie.

As Ulric approached Appleton Station he had difficulty judging just where the platform began. He thought about breathing out his special dragon breath and illuminating his surroundings, but he only had enough hydrogen in his body for three spits of fire and he wanted to save them. As if reading his mind the Falcon, with his perfect night vision, flew onto the very end of the station platform.

'We've never been here before,' whispered Ulric. 'Look, there's a long seat over there, I could do with a rest.'

'You mustn't. We should go home now,' warned the Falcon.

'Oh no,' cried Ulric, 'I want to wait for a train. I've only ever seen them from a distance. Also I've got a feeling that this is the place I'll meet the one with love in her heart for me.'

The Falcon stared at his friend before saying, 'Promise not to move about, you are well hidden here in the dark. Keep still while I take a look around.'

He never used to be so bossy, thought the Dragon, walking slowly along the platform. As his eyes adjusted he saw a thin beam of light coming towards him. He jumped at it and heard a scream. The scream frightened him. Hurrying back to where he'd been told to wait he almost fell off the edge of the platform. The Falcon was there in a flash.

'What are you doing? If you want to stay here

you're going to have to hide, jump down here and get behind these bushes.'

Ulric reluctantly did as he was told.

Because it was so dark no one was allowed on the station platform. Sophie and her mother waited at the front of the station with some other people.

'Someone reckons they have seen a dragon,' shouted one lady.

'A dragon, is it true mummy?' asked Sophie, pulling at her mother's arm.

'It'll be children dressed up,' answered Maggie, stroking her daughter's head.

'Can we see?' cried Sophie, pulling Maggie's sleeve.

'Poppet, we can't go onto the platform. Because it is so dark they're not letting us into the station.'

'Let's hope the dragon comes to see us then,' answered Sophie.

'I'm not well hidden in this holly bush,' cried Ulric.

The Falcon didn't answer.

'This bush is prickly and it's too small,' moaned Ulric, 'which part of me shall I hide?'

'Keep as still as you can,' called the Falcon, 'the train is approaching.'

Four brightly lit carriages hedeler'derd their way into Appleton station. A dozen people stepped from the train. Ulric and the Falcon watched in silence as the train pulled away.

'Daddy, Daddy,' shouted Sophie, flinging herself into his outstretched arms.

'Have you seen any dragons?' she asked, her little face turned upwards waiting for a kiss.

'No I haven't my princess, I expect they've all gone home for their supper.'

'Let's hurry home, its getting colder,' said Maggie.

'Daddy, where are your gloves?'

'I've got them here. Oh, I've dropped one.'

With the aid of the torch they searched the ground.

'I had them both when I got off the train, it must be on the platform.'

They walked towards the station.

'Sorry sir, unless you're travelling I can't let you through,' said the Station Master.

'But I've dropped one of my gloves. We've got a torch,' said David.

'Well be careful. There's all sorts of high jinx going on tonight. One of our guards saw a terrifying shadow earlier.'

After promising to be careful the three of them were allowed to retrace David's steps. Within a minute they'd walked almost to the end of the platform and Maggie found the lost glove.

'Home now,' shouted David.

'Can I hold the torch?' asked Sophie.

'Only if you keep tight hold of my hand as well,' said her mother.

Holding Maggie's hand, Sophie shone the torch across the track to the opposite platform, she made the beam of light dance along a sign that spelt out Appleton in big black letters. Turning round she let the torch light go as far as it could, it flickered over the holly bush. Sophie squealed.

'Daddy, look, there's something in those bushes,' she yelled, trying to hold the torch steady.

Maggie and David strained to see and they also saw something move.

'Don't shine the light on it poppet, it may be a fox,' said Maggie.

'It's bigger than any fox,' said David.

'What is it, what is it? cried Sophie, 'look, it's got a tail like a dragon,' she screamed excitedly.

Ulric knew he had been seen. He also knew that it was the little girl who loved him.

Pulling himself out of the holly bush, he stood

up as tall as he could and waved his tail at them.

'Goodness me,' yelled Maggie.

Sophie and David continued to stare.

Thrilled to be so close to the one with unconditional love in her heart, Ulric reared up on his hind legs. Using all the hydrogen he had been saving Ulric spat out a spectacular long plume of

Ulric retreated at great speed down the railway track

fire. Sophie squealed with delight.

'This way. Now,' shouted the Falcon.

Ulric knew he had to go. Run as fast as he could. Turning, he retreated at great speed down the railway track.

Maggie held tightly onto Sophie's hand. Sophie was unaware that her Daddy had knelt down and wrapped her in his arms. The three of them watched the large dragon shape disappear into the night.

Maggie spoke first, 'Was that, was that what I think it was?' she whispered.

'Some Halloween prank,' answered David, squeezing his daughter.

Sophie shook her head. 'That was real.' She spoke confidently, 'It was the ancient dragon from my picture book. The one who lives in a cave with the Falcon. He's probably here too,' she added, looking into the night sky.

Two

Oaktree Crossroads

Palmiro was impetuous, he was also tired. He glided to the ground, landing clumsily with a thud. Folding his sore wings, he wondered where he was.

As luck would have it he'd landed at a crossroads. Palmiro gleefully waved his tail, he was on track. His Uncle Ulric's directions had mentioned a crossroads in the middle of a wood. Now all he had to do was to follow the south-westerly route. Palmiro studied the four pathways. None indicated which way was which. Realising he'd failed to take a proper note of his bearings, he stamped his feet and began to blow large smoke rings through his nostrils. He shouldn't have raced ahead. He remembered his father shouting,

'There's no race. Palmiro, come back and fly with me.'

'But Dad, I'm longing to see Uncle Ulric,' he'd replied.

Now he was lost, he should have listened.

Palmiro arrived at a crossroads

I can't be that far way, he reasoned, I've been flying for over half a day.

From the branch of an Oak tree a Brown Owl was watching him. A young golden dragon, thought the Owl, and he's lost. The Owl knew that immature dragons have little sense of direction, unless that is, they are within sniffing distance of something familiar. Looking across the landscape the Owl saw another dragon in the evening sky. It was far away heading south-west, and for a few moments its majestic silhouette was etched across the face of the full moon. The Owl looked down at Palmiro, who was now jumping round in circles. Apart from the noise he was making nothing else stirred. Rabbits and voles were staying underground, they could undoubtedly smell dragon. I won't get any supper tonight, thought the Owl, selfishly.

Remembering a game he'd played at dragon nursery, Palmiro stood at the centre of the crossroads, lifted his tail as high as it would go before throwing it. The moment it fell, he looked over his shoulder to see where it pointed. The spade of his tail was equidistant from two of the pathways. So he tried again.

He'll work out in a minute that it can only land behind him, thought the Owl, as he watched

Palmiro's antics. After ten attempts, a despondent Palmiro gave up. The thudding of his tail was replaced by the whistle of the wind. A north wind, acknowledged the Owl, as he walked sideways into the shelter of the tree. He knew snow was coming; he began to feel sorry for the young dragon.

Palmiro began to shiver. 'I'm cold, I'm hungry, and my wings hurt,' he wailed. Like all young male dragons he wasn't very good at feeding himself. His mother always provided his food, in fact his mother did most things for him, like making his bed and ensuring he washed himself properly. Palmiro wished his mother was with him now. She would find him some food and stop his wings from hurting. He sniffed around. Unable to smell anything remotely edible he stepped into a deep ditch by a hedgerow. Perhaps if I rest, my wings will get better, he thought, before lying down. The wind quickly covered him with dry leaves. Although tired, sleep did not come easily – he was kept awake by the loud rumble of his empty tummy. Even the Owl heard it, at first mistaking it for the rumble of thunder.

Soon the snow arrived. Blankets of it came riding in on the chill north wind, swirling and dancing to an icy tune few could hear. The Owl took shelter in the hollow of the tree trunk, and chewed on the remains of last night's supper. He watched the large snowflakes settle.

Within half an hour the young dragon was asleep, and covered by a thick blanket of snow. Just his nostrils poked out. He'll be warm enough, thought the Owl. I'll try to help him in the morning, he decided, before closing one eye.

'Erasmo!' cried Ulric in delight, 'You look worn out. Come inside, come. I have prepared us a feast.'

Erasmo flew into Ulric's cave, and looked round for his son. Fading embers illuminated an empty chamber.

'Is Palmiro resting?' he asked.

'Palmiro?' replied Ulric, 'He's not here.'

'But he flew ahead of me, he should have arrived ages ago,' cried Erasmo.

'Now don't worry. He'll turn up.'

'But the sun was low in the sky when I last saw him,' replied Erasmo, pacing the marble floor.

'Perhaps he's stopped somewhere for a rest. The exuberance of youth and all that. Stop worrying – he'll find his way here,' said Ulric, in an attempt to calm his half-brother.

As they began to eat, the Peregrine Falcon

swooped into the cave. Erasmo jumped. The Falcon flew towards them and, to Erasmo's surprise, landed on a rock close to Ulric.

'Erasmo, meet my best friend, the Falcon. We share this cave. He keeps me on the straight and narrow,' added Ulric, winking at the Falcon.

'I'm very pleased to meet you,' said Erasmo, admiring the brown-and-cream feathered bird with bright yellow legs. 'Do you have a name?'

The Falcon stared at Erasmo, no creature had ever asked him if he had a name before. Sensing the Falcon's thoughts, Ulric said, 'My delightful friend doesn't have a name, for he is a free and noble spirit.

'I see,' said Erasmo.

The Falcon swivelled his head, he liked Ulric's words, and the suggestion about his free and noble spirit.

'Forgive me, dear Falcon,' said Erasmo, 'I am rather anxious tonight. I had expected my son, Palmiro, to be here already. He flew ahead of me.' Erasmo began to pace the floor again.

'You are tired Erasmo. Go into my sleeping chamber and try to get some rest,' instructed Ulric, 'We'll stay here and keep a lookout for young Palmiro.'

Erasmo, exhausted by the journey, did as he was told.

Forty miles away, the Owl, who had been watching over Palmiro, was setting off in search of food. It had stopped snowing and the landscape sparkled in the moonlight. The Owl took his time flying from one familiar tree to the next. Hearing excited noises he went to investigate. Some badgers were having fun in the snow. Three youngsters were sliding down a steep bank, under the guidance of their father. The Owl hooted, before swooping down to take a closer look.

'They've never seen so much snow,' said their father, 'I'll never get them home!' The young badgers were squealing with delight.

'We weren't going to come out tonight,' he continued, 'we heard that a dragon had landed nearby.'

The Owl blinked one eye before replying. 'Yes, a young golden dragon landed right in front of me, at Oaktree Crossroads.'

'It's true then?'

'He's sleeping now, but he's lost.'

'Lost,' repeated the badger, 'then I'd better hurry my cubs home.'

'But you mustn't fear a young dragon,' declared the Owl, 'he'd never harm you.'

'But they breathe fire.'

'Only to defend themselves,' replied the Owl, or to show off, he thought to himself.

'You seem to know a lot about dragons.'

'I do,' admitted the Owl, 'I do.'

Back at the cave the Falcon could sense Ulric's anxiety.

'I could go and look for Palmiro,' he said, as they stared into the night sky.

Ulric sniffed, and said, 'There's snow in the air. I fear my nephew could get terribly lost once the landscape becomes white.'

'I could search for Palmiro,' repeated the Falcon.

'I sense a blizzard,' said Ulric.

'I can look after myself in a blizzard,' said the Falcon, drawing back his wings.

Once airborne the Falcon cut through the wind, puffing out his chest feathers as he entered the icy air. Flying against the wind he rode its switchback currents, diving under its stronger gusts. He looked, thought Ulric, like a tiny black anchor swooping across a darkening sky.

The Badger was heading home with his cubs.

'You should come and take a look at this sleeping dragon,' said the Owl. 'You can't go through life being frightened of these rare, magnificent creatures.'

'But what if he wakes?' asked the Badger.

'Then he'll be as frightened of you as you are of him. Take those cubs of yours home. I'll wait here for you.'

Soon the Owl and the Badger were racing through the snow-covered woods. They disturbed a pair of young fallow deer who darted off in the opposite direction. Arriving at Oaktree Crossroads the Owl flew onto a nearby tree and pointed with his wing.

'Is that him?' asked the Badger, staring at Palmiro's snout which was poking out of the snow.

The Owl nodded his head. With great care the Badger crept forward. He gasped when he saw the size of Palmiro's nostrils. Then he noticed the tip of a red tongue peeking out from his golden lips. The Badger relaxed. He thought about one of his own cubs, who always slept with his tongue peeking out. The Owl and the Badger stared at the slumbering dragon.

'How large is he?' asked the Badger.

'He's still fairly small,' replied the Owl, 'he'd make about ten of you.'

'Ten of me,' shouted the Badger, jumping backwards.

Palmiro stirred and lifted his head a little. His eyelids flickered and he yawned. The Badger had never seen such a big mouth, he shot across to a tree and hid behind it. A sleepy Palmiro groaned and turned over. His snow blanket moved with him as he settled into his cosy ditch.

'You said he's lost,' whispered the Badger. 'If one of mine were ever to get lost, I would be frantic with worry. Is there anything we can do to help him?'

'I expect his family will be searching for him,' answered the Owl, 'but we could gather some food for when he wakes.'

Heading north the Falcon was facing the worst of the blizzard. Its icy fingers tore through his feathers and he knew he'd have to take shelter. Seeing some rocks scattered along the hillside he darted towards them. I'll shelter here, he thought, squeezing himself between two enormous stones. As he waited for the worst of the blizzard to pass, he hoped Palmiro had had the sense to find shelter too. Morning can't be that far away now, thought the Falcon, I'll have a better chance of finding

Palmiro during daylight. Screened from the icy blizzard he closed his eyes.

From his high branch the Owl saw dawn approaching. Beneath him the Badger was busy collecting food for the sleeping dragon.

'Do you think he'll eat earth worms and grubs?' he asked.

'He'll be grateful for anything,' replied the Owl.

Hearing voices Palmiro began to move. These were unfamiliar voices. Half asleep he wondered where he was. His nostrils twitched, he could smell food. Remembering he was alone and lost he jumped up and shook himself. Snow flew everywhere. Some landed on the Badger. Palmiro and the Badger faced each other. Palmiro saw the Badger's large claws and backed away.

As he did, the Badger crept forward and pushed all the food he had collected towards Palmiro. Forgetting his manners for a moment, Palmiro jumped at the food and gobbled it up. The Badger and the Owl watched him. When every morsel was gone, Palmiro stretched his upper body.

'My wings ache,' he called, looking round for someone to comfort him.

The Badger and the Owl looked at each other.

'I'm lost,' said Palmiro, 'LOST,' he cried loudly.

The Owl flew down and settled close to Palmiro. He could see he had tears in his eyes.

'Maybe we can help you,' said the Owl.

'I'm supposed to be at my Uncle Ulric's,' cried Palmiro, 'and my wings ache from flying too quickly, and I don't know where I am.'

'Please don't cry,' said the Badger, moving closer, 'we'll help you.'

Palmiro studied the Badger's striped body and asked, 'Can you fly?'

'No,' said the Badger, shaking his head.

'But I can,' said the Owl, stretching out a sturdy wing, 'and many of my friends can too.'

The Owl soon enlisted the help of several assorted fliers. A pair of Swifts, a Jackdaw, a Woodlark and the local Heron. They were all told about Palmiro's plight, and the need to find the home of his elderly Uncle who was called Ulric. None of the birds had heard of Ulric, but they all wanted to help. The Owl was confident one of them would find the whereabouts of Ulric's cave. The other important requirement was to make Palmiro's wings better. The Badger said that Mrs Badger had some healing balm, and he raced home to fetch it. As the snow began to melt the Owl told Palmiro to move himself into the woods, and to keep his wings as warm as possible.

As the sun began to rise the Falcon woke. Freeing himself from the rocks he stretched, shook himself, then flew high into the morning sky. A female Skylark, flying vertically, danced around him.

'I'm searching for a young dragon. A lost dragon, his name is Palmiro,' shouted the Falcon, 'his Father and Uncle are worried about him.'

The Skylark sang back, she had a sweet voice, she said she'd search for him too. Spiralling downwards she skilfully parachuted to the ground. After watching her, the Falcon took his bearings from the early morning sun and headed north east, casting his eye over acres of frozen marsh land.

Back at Ulric's cave Erasmo woke early. He'd slept fitfully, his dreams peppered with visions of a lost and injured Palmiro. He must be cold and hungry, thought Erasmo. I do hope he's safe. Then he wondered if Palmiro would decide to fly home. So he woke Ulric.

'How will I know if he decides to fly home?' he asked.

'It may be his only sensible option,' yawned Ulric.

'But he isn't sensible,' cried Erasmo, shaking his head.

'Then he won't,' replied Ulric.

At Oaktree Crossroads the Owl had gone to meet the Heron, who had some news. The Badger had applied the healing balm to Palmiro's wings and they were beginning to feel better.

'If I fly north I think I could find my way home,' said Palmiro, 'I can't stay here. Perhaps that's what I should do.'

'You ought to wait a while,' advised the Badger. 'We may get some good news soon.'

Palmiro listened and agreed. He liked someone else to make the decisions for him. And, as much as he wanted to be grown up, he had come to realise that growing up is something that has to happen gradually. He thought about his father and how worried he would be. Palmiro decided that in the future he would always listen to any advice his father gave him, even boring advice.

The Owl returned and when he saw that Palmiro was resting, he called to the Badger.

'I've heard some bad news,' he said, shaking his head. 'Both the Heron and the Jackdaw have told me that they found some old dragon bones, in a field, not far from here – I hope it isn't Palmiro's uncle.'

'Are you going to tell him?' asked the Badger.

The Owl was wise and said, 'I think we'll wait until the Swifts and the Woodlark return – in case they have other news.'

'Tell me what?' asked Palmiro, opening his eyes.

'I've got some inconclusive news,' replied the Owl.

'Inconclusive,' repeated Palmiro, 'what does that mean? Please tell me what you know.'

The Owl told Palmiro that some dragon bones had been found. But they were old bones and it was unlikely they belonged to his uncle. Palmiro began to cry. Big tears trickled down his golden cheeks.

'Don't be sad, we may have better news soon,' said the Owl.

'But they found dragon bones,' sobbed Palmiro, wondering what to do.

It was just after midday when the Woodlark returned to Oaktree Crossroads.

'I met a young Skylark today,' he said, 'she sang me the prettiest tune. Told me that a Peregrine Falcon was searching the area for a lost dragon. A dragon called Palmiro.'

'That's me,' shouted Palmiro, leaping into the air.

'There you are!' shouted the Owl. 'I told you not to dwell on gloomy thoughts,' said the Owl, adding, 'you should never think gloomy thoughts. It does you no good.'

'So what happens now?' asked the Badger.

The Woodlark said, 'I told the Swifts exactly what the Skylark sang to me and they've gone to search for the Falcon. When they find him they'll bring him here.'

'They will find him, won't they?' asked Palmiro.

'I think they will,' said the Owl.

So they all waited as patiently as they could.

Ulric meanwhile was trying to calm Erasmo's fears.

'Please relax,' said Ulric, 'worrying won't help. And it's good news that the Falcon hasn't returned. If I know him it means he's on to something.'

By late afternoon the pair of Swifts arrived at Oaktree Crossroads accompanied by the Falcon.

'I'm here. I'm here!' shouted Palmiro, waving his tail.

Not fearing dragons, the Falcon landed close to Palmiro and admired his golden scales.

'First things first,' said the Owl offering the

Falcon and the Swifts a drink of water from the hollow at the bottom of his tree.

'Have you travelled far?' asked the Owl.

'A fair distance,' answered the Falcon, 'but I'm happy to have found you, Palmiro,' he said, turning to look at the handsome young dragon, who, he thought, looked very much like his father.

'Falcon, are you tired?' asked Palmiro, admiring the Falcon's bright eyes and wonderful yellow legs.

'I am weary,' admitted the Falcon, 'but I need to get you back to your father, he is worried about you.'

'You could ride on my back,' said Palmiro, 'I'm rested now and my wings are better.'

'What a good idea,' said the Owl.

After taking another drink they were ready to go. All the birds who had helped sat in the branches of the Oak tree.

'I want to thank you all for helping me,' said Palmiro, 'and you, for your wisdom,' he said, looking at the Owl. Then turning to the Badger he said, 'And thank you for making my wings better. Maybe one day when I'm bigger, as you can't fly, I'll return and give you a ride on my back.'

The Badger didn't know what to say, and the Owl hooted with laughter.

At last they were ready to go. The Falcon hopped

onto Palmiro's back and told him to head to where the sun was setting. After a running start they were airborne.

'Bye-bye, everyone,' called Palmiro, as he flew above the treetops.

'Take good care,' shouted the Owl, as he watched the two of them climb even higher.

Three

Choosing a Name

Under the watchful eye of his father, Palmiro slept. It had been two nights since, guided by the Falcon, he'd safely arrived at his Uncle Ulric's.

'I didn't know a young Dragon could sleep for so long,' said the Falcon, who had positioned himself on a ledge just above his new friend.

'Falcon, I'll never be able to thank you enough,' said Erasmo, for the umpteenth time. 'If you hadn't found Palmiro, he would still be hopelessly lost.'

'I doubt it,' replied the Falcon, sharpening a talon, 'he'd made several friends.'

'All's well that ends well,' piped Ulric, from his favourite rock-chair. He was beginning to wonder how long Erasmo and his son were going to stay. His cave was large enough, but having guests to stay was tiring. The Falcon was also wondering how long Erasmo and Palmiro would stay, he was enjoying their company.

Erasmo, Ulric's half-brother, was much younger

than Ulric, and much less set in his ways. He was, among other things, trying to talk Ulric into having a holiday with them. He kept putting his scaly arm round Ulric.

'I wish you'd fly north, and stay with us Ulric. You'd be most welcome, along with your Falcon friend too,' he added, looking at the Falcon.

Ulric rubbed his ear. 'I don't fly great distances any more. My wings have lost their strength and power; flying further than a few acres makes me ache all over. Besides, I like my own bed at night.'

'That's a lot of excuses,' said Erasmo, and he winked at the Falcon.

The Falcon liked the idea of staying somewhere different, seeing new places, and he said so to Ulric, who answered him by snorting.

'You see, Ulric,' said Erasmo, raising his arms in the air, 'Your friend would like to take a holiday with us. Do say you'll come. Zephyrine would be delighted to have you to stay. She's always been fond of you.'

'Ah, the beautiful Zephyrine,' cried Ulric. 'Your adorable Zephyrine.'

'Who's Zephyrine?' asked the Falcon.

Palmiro was beginning to wake, he stretched slowly – starting with his head and neck, then his arms and torso, his hind legs and finally his long, scaly tail.

'Zephyrine is my mother,' he yawned.

'What a beautiful name she has,' said the Falcon.

Erasmo puffed out his chest, and said, 'It means the west wind.'

'Do all names have meanings?' asked the Falcon, who had been secretly wishing he had a name.

'Yes, most do,' answered Ulric, who knew that his name was composed of the elements of wolf and power.

Erasmo waved his arm in the air. 'Falcon, you should have a name! I can't keep calling you Falcon.'

'He doesn't need a name,' said Ulric, shuffling across the cave to put another log on the fire. 'You don't want a name, do you?'

'Perhaps I had a name once,' said the Falcon wistfully, 'maybe my mother gave me a name.'

'Can't you remember it?' asked Palmiro, leaping from his bed.

'No,' said the Falcon, lowering his head. And they could all see that he looked rather sad.

Erasmo stood up to his full height, waved his arms in the air and said, 'Lets make today the day we find you a name. I happen to know of many names that would suit a fine Peregrine Falcon like yourself.'

'We'll find you the best name,' shouted Palmiro.

'It would be interesting to have a name,' agreed the Falcon, 'although it will take a bit of getting used to.'

Ulric stopped shuffling, turned and said, 'Whatever your name becomes I will still call you Falcon.'

'Uncle Ulric,' cried Palmiro, 'your friend should have a name. Those two creatures you used to tell me stories about had names. Their names meant everything to me.'

'Ah, you mean Bugwig and Seabag,' said Ulric, smiling.

Palmiro ran over to his uncle, stood in front of him and asked, 'They were true stories, weren't they Uncle Ulric?'

Ulric patted Palmiro's shoulder, and said, 'Of course they were true.'

After hugging his uncle, Palmiro ran across to the table to have some breakfast.

Beckoning to the Falcon, Palmiro asked, 'Would you like us to find you a name?'

The Falcon landed on Palmiro's upper arm, rubbed his head against the young dragon's scaly neck. Erasmo was deep in thought. He was sitting on one of the more comfortable rocks, with his arms folded.

'Of course we'd have to perform a naming ceremony,' he said, 'being given a name is a significant event.'

While he finished his breakfast, Palmiro told his father how the Falcon had guided him safely back to Uncle Ulric's cave. As the Falcon flew from the cave Palmiro sighed and said, 'He's very special.'

Flying low through layers of winter mist the Falcon darted left then right gathering speed. His thoughts were about owning a name. He didn't know many names and wondered how they would find one for him. It would feel strange to have a name. He'd have to get used to being called by it, and the name would have to get used to him. He thought how suited Ulric was to his name, and Palmiro and Erasmo to theirs. He liked names that ended with the letter 'o', and thought he'd like his own name to end like that. Such names appeared to echo.

He circled the silent quarry before flying back to the others. It was fun having dragons to stay, he thought, dragons who made exciting suggestions, like having a name, and taking a holiday. When Ulric and I do visit them, he thought, I'll be able to announce my name, introduce myself properly. He knew that secretly Ulric would like to journey north and stay with Erasmo and his family. But he also knew that Ulric could no longer fly far because of his old wings.

There was a lot of chatter in the cave when the Falcon returned. Even Ulric looked animated.

'Ah, there you are,' said Erasmo, jumping to his feet, 'We've chosen three names, all highly suitable.'

Palmiro jumped up, and shouted, 'I know which one is the best.'

'Ssschhh!' said Erasmo, placing a claw to his lips.

Eager to hear the names they had chosen, the Falcon flew towards them.

He settled on a rock opposite Erasmo, between Ulric and Palmiro.

Erasmo coughed, as if to get their attention, then said,

'The names we've chosen are: ' "Finnian". It is of Gaelic origin and means fair. Your colouring is fair, so it would be fitting.'

So a name has to fit, thought the Falcon, scratching his ear.

'Then we thought of "Corrado". This name was favoured by royal Italians in the Middle Ages. It signifies wise and bold.'

'Corrado,' repeated the Falcon, and he listened as it softly echoed around the cave.

'And finally, we all like the name "Horatio",'said Erasmo. 'A noble name if ever there was one. Possibly of Etruscan origin.'

The Falcon blinked; 'Horatio,' he repeated.

'So what do you think?' asked Palmiro.

'I don't know,' replied the Falcon.

'Shall I tell you which I like the best?' asked Palmiro. And before the Falcon had time to answer, Palmiro jumped up and shouted, 'Corrado'.

The Falcon swivelled his head and listened to the echo, and said, 'I like them all. I particularly like Horatio and Corrado.' He looked at his friends, 'Maybe you should choose for me.'

Ulric was sharpening his claws on a rock, 'Whatever name you have it will take some getting used to,' he said. 'And I won't always remember that you've got a name at all. I will still call you Falcon.'

'When it's just you and me, it doesn't matter,' answered the Falcon, 'but I will enjoy introducing myself to others who have names.'

'What about deciding tomorrow,' said Erasmo, 'and then, as the sun sets we can begin the ceremony.'

Ulric scratched his chest and yawned. He hadn't

slept well the night before and it had been a long day.

'After supper I'll be ready for my bed,' he announced.

'But Uncle Ulric, I was hoping you'd tell me one of those Bugwig and Seabag stories before bed.'

'Were you now?' sighed Ulric.

'Oh, please Uncle, just one short story,' pleaded Palmiro.

Ulric's eyes began to twinkle. He looked at Palmiro and whispered, 'There's no such thing as a short story.'

After a splendid supper of roasted tree roots and sweet chestnuts, Palmiro called to the Falcon,

'Fly to the top of the cave, I want to shout each name to you.'

The Falcon flew to the highest ledge.

'Corrado,' called Palmiro. Again the name Corrado echoed around the cave.

'Finnian,' shouted Palmiro. A faint echo followed.

'Horatio,' called Palmiro. This name appeared to echo longer than the others.

'Corrado,' Palmiro called again. 'I want you to be called Corrado,' he said, 'because to me you are wise and bold.'

Wise and bold, thought the Falcon. Me, wise and

bold. I have never thought of myself in those ways. He looked down at Palmiro, who was yawning.

'Come along, time for bed,' said Erasmo, 'Your uncle has been remembering another story for you.'

'Please make it a long story Uncle. I'm not really tired,' cried Palmiro. He ran across to his bed, the smoothest most comfortable piece of rock in the entire cave, and jumped on it. His father covered him with some dried leaves and twigs.

'Get yourself snuggled down,' said Ulric, 'then I'll tell you the story of how Seabag and Bugwig first met.'

'I haven't heard this one,' cried Palmiro.

The Falcon, who had never heard Ulric tell a story before, swooped down too. When they were all settled next to Palmiro's bed, Ulric began.

'About two hundred years ago I met a sea turtle who could fly. Not only could this magnificent creature fly through the water but he could also fly through the air. His name was Seabag and he was hundreds of years old.

One day, while resting high up on a rock, Seabag looked down into the clear blue waters of the Indian Ocean and saw a young Manta Ray. Seabag knew by the way the Ray was swimming that it was in trouble, so he flew from his rock and dived into the sea. The Manta Ray was wary of Seabag. Sensing this, Seabag swam round him in circles. Noticing the Ray was less than a year old and exhausted, Seabag invited him to ride on his back. The Ray looked at Seabag, studied the unique pattern on his weathered face before climbing onto his warm shell. Swimming with great care Seabag carried the Ray to a shady rock pool. Sliding from Seabag's back the little Ray felt safe in the shallow waters.

'Rest here,' said Seabag, 'You are out of harm's way.'

The Manta Ray closed his small eyes, he was tired. Seabag watched him go to sleep and wondered where his family were. After a while the Ray woke up and told Seabag that he had got separated from his mother and brother. He said that they'd become entangled in a fishing net, and he, being the smallest, had managed to escape. While telling this to Seabag the Ray began to cry.

Seabag could sense the little Ray's sadness and said he would go and search for his family. The sea turtle was strong enough to destroy any fishing nets, even the wire ones. After getting some idea of where the Rays were trapped, Seabag set off.

Out in the ocean a storm was brewing. Seabag

swam beneath the choppy waves.Without warning he came across a small fishing net that was being pulled and twisted by the current but it was empty, so on he swam. To get his bearings he swam towards the surface of the sea, poked out his large head and saw a cove in the distance. That's where they will be, he thought to himself. And sure enough as he approached the cove he saw the longest fishing net he had ever seen.

Disturbed by the storm, the net was thrashing around. A great number of fish were trapped in it, many had already died. Seabag knew he'd have to move fast. Using his horny bill, which was as good as any set of teeth, he began to cut through the net, freeing fish as he did so. Methodically, he continued to destroy the net while looking for the Manta Rays. He hated nets like these. Working speedily he freed a Swordfish and it swam back to help. Working together they made good progress. Within minutes Seabag came across the long thin tail of a Manta Ray. The Ray had similar markings to the one he had placed in the rock pool. Trapped next to him was a large female who was very still.

Seabag cut the net round the smaller Ray, once free it swam to its mother. Next, Seabag moved himself underneath the female so he could bear her weight on his back. One of her pectoral wings was caught, so he asked the Swordfish to carefully cut the net above her. She remained motionless and Seabag wondered if she were still alive. The little Ray kept touching his mother, as if willing her to live. But she didn't move. Seabag continued to balance her on his back. As the Swordfish freed her, Seabag realised he was supporting her whole body weight. The little Ray remained close and the turtle sensed his distress. Seabag didn't know what to do. He watched the Swordfish freeing the last few fish. Then something unexpected happened, Seabag thought he felt the Ray move. Keeping perfectly still he felt another movement and, out of the corner of his eye saw that she was trying to raise her injured pectoral wing. Slowly she lifted both wings and propelled herself backwards, Seabag continued to support her until she slid gently from his back. He turned to watch. She was unsteady at first, then moving gracefully she swam to where her young son was waiting. He knew that her wing would heal and she would recover from the shock of being caught in a net. Thank goodness they had freed her in time. Seabag watched with a happy heart as the Rays swam away. He had an idea where they were heading, and, thought it best to return to the rock pool and tell the little Ray that both his mother and brother were safe.'

Palmiro's eye's were now closed.

'So is the little Ray called Bugwig?' asked the Falcon, who would have liked Ulric to continue the story.

'He is. And I'll finish the story another night,' promised Ulric.

Much later, long after the dragons were asleep, the Falcon was still thinking about names. By this time tomorrow I will have my name, he thought. It was this exciting thought that kept him from going to sleep.

Four

The Naming Ceremony

The Falcon watched the three dragons as they slept. Ulric was at the front of the cave, sleeping with his mouth open.

Further along, in the warmest place where the cave curved, slept Palmiro. Erasmo was further in still, sleeping in Ulric's bed. The cave was bathed in moonlight. Ulric groaned noisily before turning over. He regretted giving his bed to Erasmo. Unable to get comfortable he sat upright.

'So you're awake, too,' he said to the Falcon.

'You know I seldom sleep the whole night,' answered the Falcon, aware that he'd hardly slept at all.

'I'm going to reclaim my bed later,' grumbled Ulric, rather loudly. Then he added, 'How long do you think they will stay with us?'

The Falcon looked at him and wondered if Erasmo had heard him.

'I thought you were enjoying their company, you

looked so happy telling Palmiro that story last night,' whispered the Falcon.

'I am enjoying their company, but I miss my bed, and my routine,' grumbled Ulric.

'You must tell Erasmo that you need to sleep in your own bed, and as for your routine, you haven't got one.'

'Haven't I?' asked Ulric, stretching out his legs.

Ulric could never stretch quietly. The Falcon saw that Erasmo was beginning to stir.

'Can't you sleep, Ulric?' called Erasmo, 'Why don't you have this bed. Your own bed,' he added diplomatically, 'and I'll sleep over there.'

Not wanting to wake Palmiro, the two dragons tip-toed past each other.

Soon all was silent again.

The Falcon studied the night clouds as they danced across the face of the moon. He listened to a group of chattering bats. He loved this time of day. Letting go, he spread his wings and caught an air current. Soaring effortlessly, he deftly turned and flew higher. He liked it when he could see both the sun and the moon.

I'll have my name today, he thought. This thought had kept him awake most of the night, as well as the suggestion that he may once have had a name.

He'd been very young when Ulric had rescued him. He thought about how worried his mother must have been. He tried to remember her but couldn't. Then he thought about the story Ulric had told last night, about Seabag and Bugwig, and wondered if Bugwig had ever seen his mother again.

There had been so much to think about during the night – sleep had been impossible. How do exciting bedtime stories help you to sleep, he wondered, as he flew back to the others. Apart from Ulric snoring, all was silent. Settling into his favourite ledge he fell asleep.

It was mid-morning before he woke. Sleepily he peered at Ulric, who was moving the piece of granite that was used as a table. The was no sign of Palmiro, nor Erasmo. Swooping down he landed on the table in front of Ulric.

'Where is everyone and what are you doing?' he asked.

'Erasmo and Palmiro have gone out, and I'm re-arranging things,' answered Ulric.

'They haven't gone home have they?' asked the Falcon, fearing the worst.

'I doubt it,' said Ulric.

They have gone home, thought the Falcon, who

was still only half awake. And they didn't wake me to say goodbye. And now I'll never have a name because they've taken my name with them. He hung his head so low that it touched his chest. Ulric was too busy to notice the Falcon's sadness. He was attempting to open a secret hiding place high up in the wall.

'What are you doing?' asked the Falcon.

'I'm looking for something,' mumbled Ulric. 'I'm looking for my emerald ring.'

'My special ring,' exclaimed Ulric, holding a sparkling green stone that was set in shiny metal. He held it to the sunlight before placing it on his claw.

The Falcon stared at it. He was just going to ask for a closer look when Palmiro flew into the cave.

'My friend, you're awake,' cried Palmiro, depositing several pieces of quartz crystal onto Ulric's table.

Next, Erasmo flew in carrying some pieces of agate.

'I thought you'd both gone home,' said the Falcon, delighted to see his friends again.

'Gone home,' repeated Erasmo, 'we won't be going home just yet,' he said, winking at Ulric.

'Stay as long as you like,' said Ulric, delighted to have his own bed to sleep in again.

'We'll stay until almost Christmas. I have to go to school after Christmas,' said Palmiro.

'So you go to school,' said the Falcon.

'I've finished my main studies but Dad wants me to stay on to learn about the origins of dragon power.'

'We happen to have one of the best schools, close to where we live,' said Erasmo. 'Both Ulric and I went there. It hasn't changed much. Ulric did very well academically. His name is carved into a rock at the school's entrance.'

'That was centuries ago,' said Ulric.

'My dear Falcon,' said Erasmo, 'we've been out gathering these for your naming ceremony.'

The Falcon looked at the rocks, some shone in the sunlight, and others were unusual shapes.

'As the sun begins to set,' said Erasmo, 'we will give thanks to its power and energy and bestow upon you a name. It has to be done properly. These rocks and crystals will be carefully positioned in line with the setting sun. The moment it sets, your name will be yours, forever.'

'So what is my name to be?' asked the Falcon.

Erasmo looked at him.

'We decided that this morning. And we feel it would be better not to tell you before the ceremony.

As you know it will be one of three names, so let it be a surprise.'

'You'll like your name, Falcon,' said Palmiro, who had been sworn to secrecy.

I had no idea so much went into bestowing a name, thought the Falcon, and he told them that he felt honoured that they were making so much effort.

'How can I repay you?' he asked.

'You've already repaid us a hundred-fold,' answered Ulric. 'You flew through that dreadful blizzard and found Palmiro. And I've lost count of the times you've helped me. There's no repayment necessary, don't even think about it.'

The Falcon felt humbled. He watched Erasmo and Ulric positioning the stones.

'I'm going out for a while,' he said, wondering what to do with himself.

'I'll come too,' shouted Palmiro.

Together they flew from the cave.

As they soared above the quarry, Palmiro asked, 'I'd like to hear how you met my Uncle.'

'It was a long time ago. Your Uncle rescued me from a cage that was almost on fire,' said the Falcon.

'Wow,' exclaimed Palmiro.

'When I was very young I was captured by a man and kept in a large cage, near some stables at the back of a castle. Occasionally the cage would be opened but I couldn't fly away as a chain would be tied around my leg.'

'That's terrible,' said Palmiro.

'I can remember that my mother used to come and see me, sometimes she brought me food. Not that I went hungry, I was well fed. One particularly windy night some burning straw blew towards me from the stables. I remember at first feeling the warmth, like the sun, then I realised I was in danger. Smoke was everywhere. It became hard to breathe. I was choking when this huge shape appeared. It was Ulric. I'd never seen a dragon before. At first I was frightened, but less so than of the fire. I somehow knew that he, Ulric, had come to save me. Quickly he bent the metal bars and pushed his tail inside – I just had the strength left to hop onto his tail. He picked me up and carried me away from the smoke.

Later when I was out of danger he asked me where home was. I couldn't remember because I'd been in the cage for so long. Ulric stayed with me while I rested. The next day I didn't know where to go and he said I could travel with him. He was kind to me. We've been together ever since.'

'That's some story,' said Palmiro. 'I wish you lived closer to us so we could see you more often.'

'I think Ulric is rather attached to his home. I couldn't imagine him moving,' answered the Falcon.

'Unless my mother persuaded him,' said Palmiro. 'We have a big home, lots of roomy caves. You'll see them when you visit.'

The Falcon thought about this, he'd never contemplated moving but he would, if Ulric wanted to. More exciting things to look forward to, he thought, as he and Palmiro flew back together.

'I think if we arrange the quartz here, and the paler shades of agate there,' Ulric was saying, 'there will be more energy for the ceremony.'

'I am going to place my ring here,' said Erasmo, and he removed his ring. It was a sparkling sapphire and was fashioned like Ulric's.

'I, too, want to use my ring,' said Ulric placing his emerald ring next to Erasmo's.

'We need to get them in line with the setting sun,' said Erasmo. 'Isn't this fun? I do like naming ceremonies.'

'What will we do afterwards?' asked Ulric, thinking of his stomach and the fact that supper would be delayed this evening.

'We'll all fly and try to catch the setting sun!' exclaimed Erasmo.

'It will take us hours,' moaned Ulric, 'I can't be doing that. The three of you can go if you like.'

'It would take a long time,' agreed Erasmo, 'instead we'll stay here and have a celebration party. We could even play some games.'

When the Falcon and Palmiro returned they hardly recognised the cave.

A great space had been made at the entrance. The whole cave had been decorated with hundreds of rocks and crystals.

'This is cool,' said Palmiro.

The Falcon didn't know what to say; he flew up to his favourite ledge, which had been left unadorned.

'Uncle,' said Palmiro, 'the Falcon has been telling me how you two first met.'

'He has, has he?' said Ulric, glancing upwards. 'He was very young when we met.'

'It was a brave thing to do Uncle, flying towards a fire. It could have been fire from an unfriendly dragon,' said Palmiro.

'There are few unfriendly dragons,' said Ulric, holding a small stone, 'I can only think of one, and he died a long time ago.'

'He was more bad tempered than unfriendly,'

said Erasmo, moving a pink coloured stone, 'although it can amount to the same thing, can't it?' he added.

'Can it?' asked Ulric, 'I hope I never become bad-tempered.'

Palmiro and Erasmo both laughed.

'I admit that I do grumble from time to time, and I can be a little set in my ways,' said Ulric.

'You are a wonderful Uncle, and brave,' cried Palmiro, hugging his uncle. 'You just need to loosen up a little.'

'Loosen up,' repeated Ulric, 'I'm far too old to loosen up,' he said, and they all laughed again.

'Let us all take a special drink,' said Erasmo, and he produced four pewter goblets filled with a drink he had made from forest fruits.

'You too, Falcon, come here and drink this elixir.'

Erasmo held up one of the ancient goblets, the stem of which was encrusted with coloured jewels. The Falcon flew onto Erasmo's arm and took a sip. Settling himself next to Erasmo he noticed that some of the small crystals had started to glow. He turned towards the sun and saw that it had begun to sink behind the distant tree-tops.

Looking at his friends, the Falcon felt a thrill of excitement.

'Ulric, this home of yours is in a good position,' said Erasmo. 'You have chosen wisely. It is perfect for the setting sun.'

'Of course I've chosen wisely, for I could not sleep in a cave that did not face west.'

'You did once,' said Erasmo.

'That was a long time ago and remember how sick I became?'

'Do Falcons, when looking for homes, have to concern themselves about north, south, east and west?' asked Erasmo.

'I don't think so,' answered the Falcon.

'I believe cardinal awareness is purely a dragon thing,' said Ulric, re-filling his goblet.

'Look at the sun,' shouted Palmiro, 'it's nearly time.'

The Falcon watched as all the rocks and crystals began to glow. Exceptional light illuminated the cave. Erasmo and Ulric reached for their rings. They glowed too. Two lasers of light, one green, one blue, danced across the walls of the cave.

Erasmo positioned himself in front of the Falcon.

'It is my great honour,' he began, 'to bestow upon you a noble name. A name you will carry for the rest of your days. A name worthy of your essence.'

They all looked at the Falcon. Erasmo and Ulric crossed the blue and green lasers of light above the Falcon's head.

Next, they pointed their rings towards the setting sun. As the greeny-blue light melted, a thin golden laser of light shone from their rings. With this they made a double circle of golden light around the Falcon.

'Now,' cried Ulric.

Erasmo spoke next: 'From this day on you will be called… Horatio.'

As the Falcon's new name was spoken, the golden laser faded and a rainbow of colours emerged.

'The four Elements have heard and now know your name,' continued Erasmo.

'Come Horatio,' he shouted, flying from the cave, 'Come, and forever be true to your name.'

The Falcon flew out behind Erasmo and Palmiro. Ulric followed.

As the last ribbon of a pink light slipped beneath the horizon, they circled the quarry. Then, flying to a clearing they landed.

'Horatio,' called Palmiro, 'how does it feel?'

'It is wonderful to have such a name,' said Horatio, 'Truly wonderful.'

'Let us head back,' said Ulric, 'and enjoy the

magic colours in the cave and eat our special feast.'
    They flew off in near perfect symmetry.

The moon watched the four of them, and smiled.

Five

The Day Before

It was the day before Palmiro and Erasmo were due to return home. Palmiro was kicking small stones against a tree.

'I don't want to go home yet,' he cried, 'I like it here. Why can't Uncle Ulric come back with us?'

Erasmo sighed. 'Your Uncle will come and stay with us one day soon.'

Palmiro thumped his tail on the ground. 'Can't Horatio come back with us?'

Erasmo sighed again. 'He's your Uncle's companion – he can't leave him all alone.'

'But I know that Horatio wants to come and stay,' cried Palmiro.

'I know that too. Come along now, let's get this food back to them.'

Palmiro shrugged his shoulders, the way that young dragons do. He looked at his father who was carrying an arm full of broccoli. Dragons, especially mature dragons, love the taste of broccoli.

When they returned to the cave, Ulric was sitting on his favourite rock. His eyes were closed and his arms folded… as he became aware of their presence he said, 'I am trying hard to picture your lovely Zephyrine. I expect she is still a beauty.'

'Indeed she is,' answered Erasmo, 'and she'd dearly love to see you Ulric. Oh won't you change your mind about coming home with us tomorrow?'

Ulric opened his eyes and shook his head.

'It's such a long, long journey, I'm fearful about flying such a distance.'

Palmiro kicked a small rock across the floor and said, 'That means you'll never, ever come.'

Horatio, the Falcon, flew to Palmiro.

'Horatio, I'll miss you so much,' wailed Palmiro.

'Don't get upset,' said Horatio. Then he looked at Ulric. He knew he was frightened of taking the long journey north. Not for the first time did Horatio marvel at the mechanics of dragon flight. It was truly amazing, he thought, that they could manage to fly at all with their sizeable bodies and rather small wings.

Erasmo was busy preparing lunch, and was roasting an assortment of nuts. He had announced that he was keeping the broccoli for suppertime. They all ate quietly. An air of sadness had descended on their last day together. Palmiro looked very miserable.

Ulric chewed slowly and looked at his relatives. He thought, if they had never come to stay, he wouldn't be about to miss them. He'd so enjoyed their company and now it was going to be quiet again. Perhaps, he thought, I don't like quiet as much as I used to.

Erasmo, too, was silent, and didn't seem to have his usual appetite. He looked wistfully towards the cave's opening and took some comfort from the fact that he'd soon be back with his beautiful Zephyrine again.

Horatio looked from one dragon to the other. He could clearly see the love that bound this family together. Love can sometimes make you sad, he thought.

Palmiro, who hadn't eaten much, asked if he could leave the table. He went to sit in a corner, and thought about his new school term. He hoped they would teach him quickly so he could leave school, and home, and return here to live with his Uncle Ulric and Horatio.

Erasmo, noticing that Palmiro's mood had lifted asked his son what he was thinking about.

'Oh, I was just thinking about when I finish school,' answered Palmiro.

'You must study hard,' instructed Ulric, 'you're an intelligent dragon, you must take full advantage of those wise dragon teachers.'

'Yes Uncle,' answered Palmiro. He jumped up from his corner and called to Horatio, 'Let's fly to the woods and play.'

Horatio thought this was a fine idea so off they went. They headed for the clearing and landed on an old tree trunk.

'I like it here,' said Palmiro, 'I like it at home too, but I like it here best of all because you and Uncle Ulric are here. I don't know any falcons at home and there's no one to tell me stories about Seabag and Bugwig.'

Horatio looked at his friend and knew he was going to miss him too.

'It will be silent after you and your father have gone,' said Horatio. They stared at each other.

'Let's gather some things – to remind you of your time here,' said Horatio. 'This wood is full of interesting things to collect.'

Soon they were picking up fir cones, acorns and sycamore seeds. Palmiro collected as many as he could hold.

'Horatio, will you fly some of the way with us tomorrow?'

'I don't think that's a good idea. Ulric will feel very sad when you've gone. I think I should stay close to him.'

'He could stop himself from being sad by coming with us,' whispered Palmiro.

'Don't be too hard on him,' said Horatio, 'it is a long flight for a dragon of Ulric's years.'

In the cave Erasmo was packing up his few possessions. Ulric was once again sitting with his arms folded and eyes closed. Erasmo looked at him. He reminded Erasmo of his grandfather, who had continued to fly all his life. Erasmo scratched his head, what was it his grandfather had taken to help him to fly? It was some kind of potion. It had clearly helped him to fly great distances. I must ask Zephyrine when I get home, he thought, knowing that she'd remember.

Erasmo coughed loudly and Ulric opened his eyes.

'I hadn't dosed off,' said Ulric, 'I was thinking with my eyes closed. It always helps these days to think with one's eyes closed. A better clarity of thought.'

'Will you be sharing your thoughts?' asked Erasmo.

'I was thinking about another story I must tell Palmiro before you leave.'

'Then you must tell him tonight, Ulric.'

'Yes, yes, I know,' answered Ulric, looking at the low angle of the sun. It will be a new moon tonight, he thought. A new moon, a new beginning.

'We're back,' shouted Palmiro, as he and Horatio flew into the cave.

Ulric looked at his nephew and felt a pang of sadness. This time tomorrow, he thought, it will be forever silent. Just me rattling around in here, and the Falcon. I know I've longed for a bit of peace and quiet, but now it's about to happen I don't know if I want it any more.

Palmiro dropped what he had gathered on the table. The acorns rolled round and round. The fir cones sat like fallen skittles in a heap. Whereas the sycamore seeds, catching the breeze lifted themselves into the air before gliding to the floor.

'So you are taking a few mementoes home?' said Ulric, pleased to see that Palmiro had wisely chosen forest seeds.

'I am,' answered Palmiro. 'At school we are taught about the power in seeds, and I want these to remind me of my special holiday.'

Ulric's eyes filled with tears, he turned away.

Horatio noticed this and said, 'Ulric, you'll have to tell me the stories about Bugwig and Seabag when Palmiro has gone home.'

Ulric quickly regained his composure and sniffed. 'I will do that,' he said.

They decided to have a rest. All, apart from Erasmo who had finished packing their few possessions – it was his turn to prepare the evening meal. In truth he had made most of the meals, but he didn't mind as he preferred his own cooking to anything Ulric tried to make.

He stared at the broccoli. The next moment his eye caught the sycamore seeds and something hit him like a thunder bolt. Yes, he thought to himself, that's it!

Not wishing to disturb the others he walked away before jumping up and down with excitement. They all felt the vibration and opened their eyes.

'Are you alright Erasmo?' called Ulric.

'I'm fine. In fact I'm more than fine and you will be too when I tell you what I have remembered,' said Erasmo, skipping towards them.

'Ulric, you can remember my grandfather, on my father's side, Thorvald. The one who lived for hundreds of years and flew almost every day?'

'Oh, the one who was in the Dragon Olympics?' asked Ulric.

'Yes, that was him. Well to keep fit and airborne

'I'm heavy and too old to fly,' said Ulric

he ate the most amazing potion. He claimed that it gave him the ability to almost defy gravity as he grew older.'

All eyes were on Erasmo.

'Is this a story, Dad?' asked Palmiro.

'It is a story, but it's a true story. Ulric, I think it could help you to fly long distances again. Maybe it could help you to come home with us tomorrow.'

'Yes, yes please,' cried Palmiro unable to contain himself.

Ulric stretched out his limbs and they cracked.

'I can't see how taking some potion will help me lift my heavy bones into the air.'

'Oh, you will think differently after you've taken it,' answered Erasmo.

'So what's in the potion?' asked Palmiro.

Erasmo picked up a handful of the sycamore seeds, then let them drop. The seeds swirled around for quite some moments before spiralling to the ground.

'Look how they ride the air,' said Erasmo. Next he excitedly pointed to the broccoli.

'We chop the broccoli and mix it up with ground sycamore seeds. Under the light of a new moon it is all stirred with a silver feather taken from a Heron.'

'It's a new moon tonight,' squealed Palmiro.
'I know,' said Erasmo, jumping into the air once more. 'Palmiro, I need you to gather some more of these sycamore seeds, and, we need to find a silver Heron feather.'

'I'll go and find the feather,' called Horatio, darting from the cave.

'I don't wish to be a spoil-sport here,' said Ulric, 'But I can't see this working for me. I'm a heavy old dragon. And I've been eating broccoli for years and, as much as I enjoy it, it doesn't help me to fly.'

'Trust me Ulric. I have a feeling this will positively propel you into the air,' answered Erasmo. 'But you must be honest with me, tell me before the others return – if this potion does help you, would you be happy to travel back with us and stay for a while? We do have comfortable rooms and beds. Our cave is weatherproof and has special heating.'

Ulric smiled. Of course he wanted to go. He longed for a more comfortable winter. And he would enjoy being pampered by Zephyrine. As if reading his mind Erasmo said, 'Zephyrine would make such a fuss of you.'

Ulric stood, 'Erasmo, the truth is that I would be delighted to come home with you. But you may learn one day when your wings haven't got the strength they used to have, that you simply can't do the things you want to. Now if this potion works, and lifts me effortlessly into the air then that would be fantastic. But if it doesn't, well, you must let me remain here and not make a fuss. I don't want to see Palmiro getting upset. Goodbyes are impossibly hard.'

'I hear what you are saying,' answered Erasmo.

Horatio was the first to return. He was carrying a long silver feather in his beak.

Erasmo was impressed, 'That was quick,' he said.

'I flew to the lake and met a young Heron who was preening himself, so I asked him for one of his feathers.'

Erasmo took the feather from him. 'This is perfect,' he said.

After Palmiro had returned with the sycamore seeds, Erasmo, using a rock, began to grind them into a powder. Palmiro, under the supervision of his father chopped up the broccoli. All was mixed together. They had to wait for the new moon to rise.

'When do I eat this potion?' asked Ulric.

'Early in the morning, just before we set off,' answered Erasmo.

'And how long will it keep me in the air?' asked Ulric.

Erasmo didn't really know the answer to this question. He hoped that if Ulric ate enough of the potion it would enable him to fly effortlessly for the whole day. But he wasn't sure. In order to instil some confidence, he said, 'It should last the whole of the day.'

'You'll be coming home with us Uncle Ulric, I know you will,' cried Palmiro, running across to embrace his uncle.

'I will if it works,' replied Ulric, hugging his nephew. 'Is that OK with you Falcon, I mean Horatio?'

Horatio swooped down and landed close to them.

'That's fine with me,' he answered.

'Hooley Dooley!' screamed Palmiro. He skipped around the cave looking from time to time at the thin new moon.'

There was lots of chatter in the cave as they ate their supper. The three dragons sat around the fire enjoying the broccoli soup that Erasmo has spiced up with a secret ingredient. As Palmiro ate his, he hoped with all his heart that the special potion would work for his Uncle in the morning. Next they tucked into roasted pine cones in a herb sauce, followed by baked apples stuffed with nuts.

'I do like these nutty apples,' exclaimed Horatio.

'Another utterly delicious supper,' declared Ulric, picking at his teeth with his longest claw.

Under the light of the new moon they each took turns to stir the special potion. The Heron's feather was as light as air itself, but amazingly strong.

The excitement had tired everyone. So they decided to go to bed extra early.

'Uncle, if we go to bed early then tomorrow will arrive quicker,' shouted Palmiro. He planted a kiss on Ulric's cheek and said, 'I'm sorry but I'm too tired for a story tonight.'

Ulric was also tired. It had been an emotionally exhausting day. Erasmo was thinking about an early night too, although he knew that he would have to get up several times to stir the special potion.

Above them Horatio settled on his favourite ledge. He looked at Ulric and wondered if he would be able to manage the long journey tomorrow. Knowing he'd been born in the north Horatio felt a thrill of excitement. His own relatives must be there somewhere, he thought, and maybe his mother. Not that he imagined he would ever see her again. Nevertheless he closed his eyes and made two wishes.

Six

Taking Flight

Erasmo rose early. He placed a bowl containing half of the broccoli and sycamore seed mixture on the table and waited for Ulric to wake up. Ulric's long tail was quivering. He was awake, although his eyes remained closed. Sensing Erasmo was watching him, and conscious of the fact he had stopped snoring, he opened one eye.

'Is it morning already?' he asked, yawning.

'It is,' whispered Erasmo.

Stretching out his tail and hind legs, Ulric grunted noisily as he sat himself on the edge of his bed. Horatio flew to him.

'Erasmo,' said Ulric, rubbing his eyes, 'When do I eat this mixture?'

'Have it now, before breakfast,' instructed Erasmo. And to speed things up he passed the bowl to Ulric.

Ulric stared at the special mixture placed in front of him. Instinctively he lifted the bowl to his nose and sniffed. Some of it went up his nostrils.

'Be careful Ulric,' shouted Erasmo. 'You are supposed to eat it, not snort it.'

Under the watchful eye of both Erasmo and Horatio, Ulric ate the mixture.

He chewed slowly and was careful not to speak with his mouth full.

'Some of this broccoli stalk is a bit tough,' he said, 'but the flavour is good.'

'Finish it and tell us how you feel,' said Erasmo.

After a few minutes Ulric had eaten it all. Erasmo gave him a drink of water.

'I don't think I feel any different,' said Ulric, walking from his bed.

'It may take a little while,' said Erasmo. 'I'm going to wake Palmiro. We must be ready to set off after breakfast.'

'So soon,' said Ulric.

Horatio had flown from the cave. He was flying quickly, circling the quarry, and wondering what the day would bring. His thoughts were mainly about Ulric. He wondered if Ulric would be able to fly as effortlessly as Erasmo said he would. I do hope so, thought Horatio, it would be special for us all to fly north together.

Horatio began to wonder about his own family.

Did they ever think about him? He believed that his mother might and for a moment he felt a little bit sad. He'd love to see her again and tell her about his life with Ulric. Explain how Ulric had saved him from that fire and how the two of them now lived together. There were lots of other stories to tell his mother too, and he wondered if that day would ever come. I must not get too excited about travelling north, he told himself, as he swooped above the chestnut coppice. And if Ulric can't manage this journey, then I must hide my disappointment.

With that thought in his mind, Horatio flew back to the cave. Palmiro was waving to him. Turning, Horatio swooped low and landed on Palmiro's outstretched arm.

'Horatio, where have you been? Quickly, come inside, come and take a look at Uncle Ulric.'

Ulric was in the middle of the cave, skipping. With each skip his whole body remained in the air for almost two seconds.

'Don't over do it, Ulric,' called Erasmo. 'Conserve your energy.'

'How can I conserve my energy? I can't stop. I can feel myself getting lighter and lighter,' cried Ulric, skipping some more.

'Let's set off now then,' cried Palmiro, jumping into the air. 'Now, while Uncle Ulric feels he can fly.'

'We haven't yet had breakfast,' said Erasmo. 'None of us should attempt a long journey on an empty stomach.'

So he and Palmiro busied themselves preparing a quick breakfast.

Erasmo told Ulric to sit down; Ulric tried but had great difficulty. He could sort of sit if he held onto the chair but his tail kept rising.

'This is a most peculiar feeling, Horatio,' whispered Ulric, 'just look where my tail is.'

Horatio had never seen Ulric's tail pointing at the ceiling before. It was a perplexing sight. Horatio hoped that his own tail would never do that to him – and vowed there and then that he'd never eat ground sycamore seeds mixed with broccoli.

'Are you looking forward to our journey, Horatio?' asked Ulric.

But before Horatio could answer, Ulric's tail fell to the floor and landed with a thump. The sound vibrated around the cave. Erasmo and Palmiro rushed to him.

'Are you alright Uncle?' asked Palmiro.

'I think I am,' he answered, rubbing his tail. 'Erasmo, why has this happened?'

Erasmo shook his head.

'I think it's your body getting used to the effects of the special potion,' he answered, although he didn't really know.

As they ate their breakfast Ulric's arms began to float above his head.

'Look at my arms,' he cried, 'they are taking themselves into the air.'

Delighted by this Palmiro waved his arms above his head too. Then with great effort Ulric managed to pull one arm down so he could finish eating his breakfast.

'I do feel odd,' he told his audience, 'all light and bouncy.'

'We'll set off soon,' said Erasmo, 'it is perfect weather for our journey.'

A wintry sun had risen. Ulric stood at the cave's edge and watched wisps of cloud being blown across the pale blue sky. Erasmo, who was the only one carrying anything, adjusted the straps on his old back-pack.

'Are you ready then Ulric?' he asked.

Palmiro and Horatio both looked at Ulric.

'I'm ready,' he said, looking back into his cave.

'I'll close your cave,' said Erasmo, pushing a sizeable boulder across the cave's entrance.

'Let's all fly over to the other side of the quarry and take our bearings from there,' instructed Erasmo.

Erasmo, Horatio noted, was clearly the one in charge.

Ulric did as he was told. He, too, was pleased that Erasmo was taking the lead. It was important to have a leader on a journey, someone who would make all the necessary decisions and keep the group together.

'Now no flying too far ahead Palmiro,' said Erasmo.

'Dad, I won't be doing that again,' he replied.

Off they set. Ulric positively glided over the quarry. At the other side they regrouped and listened as Erasmo suggested that they flew north until the sun was just a dragon's breath above the horizon, then, he said, they'd take a rest.

'Now if at any time one of you wishes to stop, snort loudly,' said Erasmo.

Palmiro looked at Horatio,

'Can you snort?' he asked.

Horatio shook his head.

'Horatio, you come and tell me if you need to take a break,' said Erasmo, 'and I'll let the others know.'

So the plan for the first part of the journey was made. Erasmo tightened the straps on his back-pack and called out, 'One, two, three.' They all left the ground at the same moment and soared high into the air. Horatio felt giddy with excitement. He'd never flown with three dragons before. This was a big adventure. This was almost the most exciting thing that had ever happened to him. Of course he would have to fly slower than normal, but he liked the thought of flying in a group.

Erasmo watched Ulric, and stayed close to him to check his progress. Horatio also looked at Ulric, and noticed he was flying without his usual huff and puff. Horatio then glanced at Palmiro, who was flying with a happy smile on his face.

'I am so pleased you are both coming home with us,' shouted Palmiro. 'I can't wait to introduce you to my friends.'

You'll introduce me to your friends, thought Horatio, how wonderful. And now that I have a name I will be able to say, my name is Horatio. Feeling carefree, Horatio stretched out his wings as far as he could and darted ahead of them all.

'Stop showing off,' shouted Palmiro.

Behind them Ulric was enjoying himself too.

'It's very odd but I don't feel heavy at all. It feels

like something is holding me up by my middle and something else is propelling me along. Two quite separate things. I am very grateful to that broccoli and those ground seeds.'

Erasmo looked at him, and saw that he was at ease in flight and silently thanked whatever had reminded him of that special potion. Isn't it odd, he thought, how something you'd almost forgotten, something buried deep in your memory can surface, just when you need it. The trigger of course was Palmiro bringing back those sycamore seeds. How amazing one's memory can be, and, in this instance how very, very fortunate.

On they flew over woods and open countryside, over small towns and villages heading north.

After a while Ulric said, 'When we stop for a rest, I do hope I will be able to fly again.'

'Of course you will,' replied Erasmo, who was a great believer in the power of positive thinking. As a precaution, Erasmo had packed the remainder of the broccoli and sycamore seed mixture. He, too, had no idea of how long the potion would work. Zephyrine would know, or her sister – between them they knew everything about mixing potions and dealing with ailments.

He sighed contentedly at the thought of seeing

her again. They only had Palmiro living with them now. Their other two sons, twins, had left home years ago and had found their own caves to live in. However, on special occasions like birthdays and family celebrations they returned home for a few days. As soon as they hear their Uncle Ulric is staying with us, they'll be home like a shot, thought Erasmo. We'll invite everyone we know and have a party, he decided.

Zephyrine loved arranging parties and she was the perfect hostess.

As the sun began to slide towards the horizon Erasmo looked ahead for somewhere to take a rest. His eyesight was excellent. Seeing some hills in the distance, peppered with large granite rocks, he called to the others.

'By my calculations we are more than half-way home. Let's take a rest and have some refreshment.'

The four of them glided down and landed on the bracken. Horatio watched Palmiro bouncing up and down on the springy ferns.

'Horatio, come and bounce on this. It's great fun.'

'I can't bounce,' said Horatio

'Yes, you can. Come over here and I'll teach you.'

Erasmo took off his back-pack and opened it. He took out three apples, then he looked at Horatio.

'I have nothing for you, Horatio, unless you'd like half an apple,' he said.

'Don't worry about me,' replied Horatio, 'I ate well this morning.'

As the dragons ate their apples, Erasmo thought about Zephyrine's exquisite cooking. His mouth watered at the thought of her pine cone pastry and rosemary flavoured nut crumble. Erasmo mentioned Zephyrine's cooking to the others and Ulric's mouth began to water.

'Stop,' he cried, 'before you have me drooling like a dog.'

'What is the meaning of these large stones set in a circle?' asked Palmiro.

'Druids used to worship here,' answered his father.

'What are Druids?' asked Palmiro.

'They were wise men and women. Mystics and philosophers who possessed great mathematical and astronomical skill.'

'Could they fly?' asked Palmiro.

'No, I don't think they could,' replied Erasmo, and with this answer Palmiro lost interest.

'Ah, the Druids,' whispered Ulric, scratching his head. 'I knew a dragon who met a Druid once. He told him that his spirit emerged from the tides of the sea and rode upon the light of the sun,' said Ulric, chewing his apple core.

Horatio could see a large lake, so after telling Erasmo, he and Palmiro flew towards it. Erasmo stayed with Ulric, who was now leaning against one of the stones with his eyes closed.

Noticing the lake was frozen, Horatio flew ahead, landed on the ice and skated.

'Hooley Dooley!' shouted Palmiro chasing after him.

Before Horatio could say anything Palmiro jumped onto the iced lake. Horatio heard it crack. He shouted but it was too late. All he could hear was the splintering sound of ice breaking as Palmiro's body disappeared into the lake. For a moment only Palmiro's hand and tail remained on the surface. Horatio let out a screech of anguish. Within seconds Erasmo and Ulric were there and watched Palmiro's tail going deeper into the lake. Breaking more ice Erasmo dived in. Horatio and Ulric watched as bubbles rose to the surface. All was then still. After several long seconds Horatio, who was walking along the edge of the broken ice, tried to speak but couldn't. He looked at Ulric.

'I'm going in too,' said Ulric, preparing to dive.

Please don't, Horatio wanted to say, but couldn't.

As Ulric got ready to dive, ice erupted around them. Erasmo emerged, clutching Palmiro tightly. Palmiro's body was limp and his eyes were closed. Ulric reached for Palmiro's tail and helped Erasmo carry him to some dry bracken. Ulric supported

Ulric and Erasmo watched Palmiro going deeper into the lake

Palmiro's body while Erasmo pummelled at his chest. A lot of water came out of Palmiro's mouth and nostrils. Coughing and spluttering, Palmiro gasped for breath. Erasmo pummelled his back, working hard to ensure all the water came out of Palmiro's lungs. Wrapping him in some dry bracken Erasmo hugged his son.

When his breathing returned to normal Palmiro opened his eyes. Horatio hovered overhead, watching his dear young friend. When Erasmo had finished hugging him he squeezed him and kissed him. Ulric did the same.

'You should never, ever walk onto ice,' said Erasmo, continuing to hug his son. 'Frozen lakes are so dangerous. You could easily have drowned – we'd have lost you forever. Thank goodness Horatio was with you.'

'But it was all my fault,' said Horatio, finding his voice at last. 'I was the one to skate across the lake. I didn't think Palmiro would follow me.'

'Don't blame yourself. Palmiro is old enough to know he should never step onto ice,' said Erasmo.

'We'll soon get him warm,' said Ulric, rubbing Palmiro's shivering body.

Erasmo dried himself on some bracken.

'Sorry,' said Palmiro weakly. 'I didn't expect the ice to break. I didn't think properly.'

'To anyone weighing more than a few pounds, an iced lake, or pond, although inviting is a most treacherous place,' said Ulric.

'Remember those wise words,' added Erasmo.

Ulric gathered together some twigs, took a deep breath, held it for a moment, then exhaled a long plume of fire. A camp-fire was quickly started and it wasn't long before Palmiro and Erasmo were dry and warm again. Taking a small, dark bottle from his back-pack Erasmo gave Palmiro a sip. "To be taken in emergencies" - was written on the label. He then took a large sip himself.

'We ought to set off shortly if we are going to get home today. Or we could find shelter and bed down here for the night,' he said.

'I'd like to carry on,' said Ulric, who, in the last hour had begun to feel a little heavier. He was keeping these thoughts to himself and trying hard to think positively as Erasmo had instructed him to do.

'I sort of feel OK,' said Palmiro, although his voice sounded weak.

Ulric could tell that Palmiro wasn't feeling strong and shook his head.

'You've had a nasty shock,' said Erasmo, putting an arm around his son 'I don't know if it would be wise to continue; what do you think Horatio?'

'I can't think straight. I still feel so responsible for Palmiro's accident,' said Horatio.

Erasmo beckoned Horatio, who flew onto his shoulder.

'There's no need to feel responsible,' answered Erasmo, stroking the Falcon's back.

'It wasn't your fault at all,' whispered Palmiro, reaching out to Horatio.

Erasmo looked around. He stared at the large stones.

'I think we should rest here. The healing energies from these stones will help to restore you, Palmiro. We will all set off again at dawn,' he said.

The sun fell quickly. And they all knew that under the circumstances this was the best plan. Palmiro would, over-night, recover his strength, but would Ulric lose his; lose his effortless ability to fly? It was a concern. Erasmo had been thinking about this. He did have the remainder of the broccoli and sycamore seed mixture in his back-pack. But would it work again? Would it be as effective? He didn't know the answer.

It's just as well none of my uncertain thoughts can reach Ulric, he thought.

Many years ago, Ulric had learned how to mind read – not that he'd been able to do so for ages. But today he could. It's that potion, he thought. It's enabled me to remember all kinds of things. Now, do I tell Erasmo that I can tell what he is thinking, he asked himself. After some thought he decided it was probably kinder not to.

Seven

Almost Home

Ulric wasn't sleeping well. The bed he'd made out of rocks and bracken was too soft for him. He turned over and looked at Palmiro, who was lying close by. Palmiro was in a deep sleep. At the other side of Palmiro, Erasmo slept too. Ulric could see into their night-time dreams. It was strange, he thought, being able to do that again.

In an effort to get comfortable, Ulric reached for a large rock to use as a pillow. Settling down again he thought about his body weight. Yesterday he'd felt so light, and had flown through the wind and rain almost effortlessly. Now, feeling heavier, he worried about the rest of the journey.

He knew from reading Erasmo's mind that Erasmo had packed the rest of the potion; but would it work again? This was the worry that was keeping him awake. Ulric knew that the healing stones would help Palmiro to recover, but their energy wasn't strong enough to help him. He turned and lay on his back. Watching the stars he wondered where Horatio was.

Erasmo had begun to snore. Ulric saw that he was sleeping with a protective arm across his son. It was just as well, thought Ulric, for he could tell that Palmiro was beginning a bad dream. A dream about being trapped underneath an iced lake. Ulric reached out and stroked Palmiro's soft, scaly back, soon the young dragon's breathing steadied. Feeling wide awake Ulric sat up and stared into the darkness. He couldn't see or hear Horatio, but he could hear an owl hooting and the cry of foxes.

'Can't you sleep, Ulric?' asked Erasmo, opening his eyes.

'I'm fully awake,' moaned Ulric, 'I think I'll go for a little stroll.'

'Don't go too far and get lost,' said Erasmo, before closing his eyes.

Get lost, I won't get lost, thought Ulric, standing up and flicking his tail.

His night vision, like all dragons', was excellent, not that he had any intention of going very far. Just far enough to take a look around and see what he could see.

Horatio, too, was taking a look around. Flying on

his own he was travelling fast. Swooping through the night sky at great speed then turning and dipping low. Horatio could fly incredibly quickly when he wanted to. As he flew he thought about the speed of dragon flight. Dragons, he decided, only appeared to have one speed, a steady speed. And their flight was always preceded with much flapping of wings. Like gulls taking off from a beach; a clumsy ascent until they got going. Now he could understand why Palmiro had, on the way down, charged ahead. He was young and full of energy – it would have been hard for him to fly along at a middling pace with his father.

Ulric meanwhile was enjoying himself. He was humming as he trampled along through unfamiliar terrain. He was sniffing too in case there was anything remotely edible in the undergrowth. He was hungry and his large tummy had begun to rumble. Horatio, hearing Ulric's tummy rumbling swooped down to greet him.

'Ulric, I thought you'd be fast asleep,' said Horatio.

'No. I have things on my mind, and besides I can't sleep when I'm not in my own bed. I hope they have a comfortable bed for me at Erasmo's,' answered Ulric.

'They will have, I'm sure,' replied Horatio. Then to cheer Ulric up he said,

'There's an interesting wood over there. I've just flown over it. Shall we go and explore it together?'

'What a fine idea,' said Ulric, who was grateful for Horatio's company.

Off they set. Ulric striding out, stamping on thin trees and bushes with his enormous feet, while Horatio wove gracefully through the tree tops.

When they reached some Sycamore trees, Ulric's nose twitched; he could smell and almost taste the seeds.

'Look, Horatio,' he called, licking his lips, 'I think I should eat some of these.' And before Horatio could say anything, Ulric stuffed a handful of sycamore seeds into his mouth. He chewed them quickly and as he did so, bent down to gather some more.

Horatio watched him, 'Do you think you should eat so many?' he asked.

'I like them,' answered Ulric, 'and I am beginning to feel a bit heavy again. They may help me.'

Horatio didn't know what to say. He sat on a low branch and waited for Ulric to finish his feast. Feeling full, Ulric sat down and picked his teeth.

'I feel lighter already,' he said, jumping up and

down. As he jumped for the third time something strange happened. He took off. His whole body began to float. Horatio could see that he wasn't flying because his wings were perfectly still. Up he went.

'Look at me,' shouted Ulric gleefully, 'I'm as light as a feather.'

Horatio stared at his companion, who continued to rise.

'Come back,' he shouted.

Ulric looked down at him and waved. Seeing how far he had risen Ulric tried to come back to the ground. He flapped his wings and tried to force his body down, but like a balloon he continued to rise.

'I can't get down,' he shouted.

Horatio could tell that Ulric was frightened. He flew towards him and told him to hold on to one of the branches. Ulric grabbed at a branch, but it snapped off.

'Horatio, quickly, sit on my head,' pleaded Ulric, 'stop me from going higher.'

So Horatio sat on Ulric's head. But it was no good, he was too light to stop Ulric rising.

'Take hold of a sturdier branch,' suggested Horatio.

Ulric grabbed at one of the main branches. He swung himself towards it. With great effort he managed to manoeuvre his body along the branch and wrap his hind legs round it too. This seemed to steady him and he held on tight. He tried coiling his tail around the branch – but his tail was rising above him like it had done before.

'Help me! What shall I do now?' cried Ulric.

'Try to stay there,' answered Horatio. He looked at the branch and knew that under normal circumstances it wouldn't hold Ulric's weight.

'I'm going to fetch Erasmo,' he said.

'Oh, don't do that,' cried Ulric. 'He'll tell me off.'

'What else can I do?' asked Horatio.

'Oh, go on then, but be quick. I don't know how long I can hold on here.'

With lightening speed, Horatio flew back to Erasmo and Palmiro.

He flapped his wings loudly until Erasmo woke up with a start.

'Whatever is the matter?' he asked, sensing Horatio's distress.

'It's Ulric. He's trapped in a tree. He's rising higher and higher.'

'Oh dear,' said Erasmo sitting up, 'Where is this tree?'

'It's about half a mile away,' answered Horatio.

Erasmo glanced at Palmiro who was sleeping

peacefully. He covered him up with more dry leaves before flying off with Horatio.

When they got to Ulric he was holding onto the highest branch.

'Hello Erasmo,' called Ulric, 'I'm in a spot of bother here,' he added.

Erasmo flew to him.

'What have you been doing? I can't understand it.' Erasmo scratched his head. 'Why on earth have you become weightless in the middle of the night. You haven't eaten anything have you?'

'I did have a small snack earlier,' said Ulric, sheepishly.

'What kind of small snack?' asked Erasmo.

'He ate a whole pile of sycamore seeds,' said Horatio.

'You did what?' asked Erasmo, hardly able to believe what Horatio had just said.

'I was hungry and I thought they'd do me good. I was feeling heavier again. I didn't want to tell you. Oh what am I going to do?'

'Stay calm,' said Erasmo, putting a hand on Ulric's shoulder. 'Now, Horatio, I need you to bring me that length of rope out of my back-pack. And check that Palmiro is still sleeping. It is important that he rests.'

Horatio flew back to fetch the rope. What would Erasmo do with the rope, he wondered. Holding the rope in his ebony talons Horatio hovered over Palmiro. Palmiro was in a deep sleep. He stroked Palmiro's head with the tip of his wing before flying back to the others.

'I don't want to be tied to a tree,' Ulric was shouting. 'At my age being tied to a tree, it's a huge indignity.'

'We are going to have to tie you to something,' said Erasmo. 'Or you'll continue to float higher and higher. We have no choice. I'll try to pull you down first and tie you to the trunk. We can't have you falling from that height.'

'Falling! I don't want to fall,' cried Ulric. 'I would break all my bones and then what would happen to me,' he wailed.

'There will be no breaking of bones,' said Erasmo, who knew that if Ulric fell and broke some of his bones it would be almost impossible to move him.

Returning with the rope Horatio gave it to Erasmo. Unravelling it Erasmo tied one end to the thickest part of the tree's trunk. He gave Horatio the other end and Horatio held it in his beak.

'Ulric, do you feel you could try to fly down?' asked Erasmo.

'I don't know. If I let go I think I'll go higher and higher', he answered.

Erasmo scratched his head, 'In that case, I will fly up and grab hold of you. And when I say so you must let go of the branch, then I'll forcibly bring you back to the ground.'

Poor Ulric was tied to a tree to stop him floating away

'What if you float up with me too?' asked Ulric, 'we'll have nothing to hold on to.'

Erasmo ignored this negative comment and said, 'First, I'm going to tie the other end of this rope around me.'

Horatio gave the end of the rope back to Erasmo,

who measured out the required length before tying the rope, with a special knot, around his middle. He told Horatio that he needed him to be standing by, as once he'd got Ulric to the ground it would be Horatio's job to take the loose rope and wrap it, as quickly as possible, several times around Ulric and the trunk of the tree.

'What if it doesn't work?' asked Ulric.

'Don't think like that. Remember the third Dragon Law: "Always think in the positive," answered Erasmo.

'I'll try,' mumbled Ulric.

Taking a deep breath Erasmo flew to Ulric. He positioned himself so that he could grab him from behind. Taking a firm hold of Ulric he shouted, 'Let go now.'

Ulric let go. The next moment the two of them floated above the top of the tree. Only the rope stopped them from floating higher. Horatio flew towards them to see if he could do anything.

'Ulric, listen to me,' Erasmo was saying, 'in a moment I'm going to use all the muscle power I have, to get you back to the ground. I may jolt you, so be ready.'

'I'm ready,' said Ulric.

Horatio watched Erasmo and could tell he was

concentrating. Sucking in as much breath as he could, Erasmo began to make a strange noise – like a deep groan. As this groaning continued Erasmo and Ulric began their combined descent. It was slow at first, and Horatio could see that Erasmo was almost wrestling Ulric to the ground. As they got lower Erasmo shouted out, 'Horatio, the rope.'

Horatio was ready. He held the slack rope firmly in his talons. Erasmo forcibly pushed Ulric to the ground and held him against the tree. Horatio, using his impressive speed whizzed round and round with the rope, securing Ulric's body against the tree's trunk.

'Phew!' said Erasmo finally letting go, 'Ulric, you're safe at last.'

'Safe,' uttered Ulric. His head slumped on his chest. He looked a sorry sight tied to the tree – the rope wrapped and knotted around his middle.

'I'm exhausted. I haven't an ounce of energy left in me. I will wither here,' he added dramatically.

Horatio flew to the ground and picked up a small, dark-green bottle.

'I also brought this from your bag,' he said, giving it to Erasmo.

'Bless you my friend,' said Erasmo. He unscrewed the top and took a sip of the 'emergency tincture'. Next, he held Ulric's jaw and dribbled some into his dry mouth. Ulric opened his eyes, then closed them again and let his head slump onto his chest.

'I'll go and check on Palmiro,' said Horatio.

'Yes,' agreed Erasmo, 'You go back. I'll stay here until Ulric feels well again,' he whispered. Horatio stared at Ulric before flying off.

'Feels well again,' repeated Ulric, lifting his head and rolling his eyes, 'I'll never be well again. I feel dreadful. I could even die.'

'You won't die,' said Erasmo, 'You've got a few hundred years left in you yet.'

Ulric moaned. Erasmo realising that he, too, felt exhausted sat himself next to Ulric and leaned against the tree trunk.

Soon Ulric body's looked less tense and he began to snore. Erasmo allowed himself to close his eyes. Soon they were both asleep.

Smudges of pink morning light bathed the horizon. Horatio could see that Palmiro was beginning to wake. Opening his eyes Palmiro asked, 'Where am I?'

Horatio flew to him and reminded him of what had happened the previous day. Then he told him what had happened to Ulric.

'Poor Uncle Ulric,' said Palmiro, sitting up and rubbing sleep from his eyes.

'Is he going to be alright? Can we go and see him?'

'We can if you are you feeling better,' said Horatio.

Palmiro stood up and stretched, he said he was feeling well again, so off they went. They both heard Ulric and Erasmo long before they saw them. Huge dragon snores echoed through the woods.

'Dad,' Palmiro whispered, as he landed next to him. Erasmo's eyelids flickered open.

'Oh, what an exhausting dream I had,' he said. 'Palmiro, Palmiro, how are you this morning?' He got up and hugged his son.

'I'm fine now. How is Uncle Ulric?'

Erasmo turned and looked at his half-brother.

'He's had a nasty shock,' he said, noticing the rope had slackened around Ulric's middle.

Ulric groaned loudly. 'It was a hundred times worse than any nasty shock,' he said, opening one eye. 'Look at me tied to this tree.' He pulled at the rope.

'Undo me,' he cried.

Erasmo held the rope, and said, 'We don't want you floating off again Ulric. Tell me how you feel.'

Ulric groaned again. 'I feel heavier than ever. I'm far too heavy to float away. And I'm too heavy to ever fly again.'

'What nonsense. You will fly again. But right now I need to know that when I untie you, you won't float away,' said Erasmo.

'I'm too heavy to float,' shouted Ulric.

'To be on the safe side,' said Erasmo, 'I'm going to sit on you while Horatio and Palmiro undo the rope.'

'Sit on me,' cried Ulric, in despair. 'Do be careful. The pain in my bones is like toothache this morning.'

Erasmo sat himself as gently as he could on Ulric's lap. Horatio and Palmiro quickly untied the rope. Realising that Ulric wasn't going to float away Erasmo stood up.

'Good. Now, Ulric try to stand,' instructed Erasmo.

Ulric pulled a face, 'I haven't got the strength,' he answered.

'Come on Uncle,' said Palmiro, and he took hold of Ulric's arm. Erasmo gripped Ulric's other arm and they tugged at him.

'You'll pull my arms out of their sockets,' cried Ulric. Then after a few huffs and puffs he stood up and leaned against the tree for support; the very tree he'd floated to the top of only a few hours ago.

'Thank goodness you are back to normal,' said Erasmo.

'I don't feel normal,' grumbled Ulric.

Horatio, noticing how tired Ulric looked, whispered something into Erasmo's ear. Erasmo shook his head. Ulric looked at the pair of them and read their thoughts.

'You are wondering whether or not to give me the rest of that special potion aren't you?' he asked, 'Well I don't want it. I don't want that floating feeling ever again. And I never ever want to be tied to another tree.'

'Then let's fly back to where we stopped for the night,' said Erasmo. Who was keen to know if Ulric could fly at all.

Ulric flapped his wings but his body refused to leave the ground. He tried again, but nothing happened.

'Oh dear,' said Erasmo.

'Uncle Ulric, take a run and move your wings like this,' said Palmiro, demonstrating one of his more enthusiastic take-off techniques.

Ulric looked at Palmiro and shook his head.

'There's only one thing that can help me now,' he said, turning to Erasmo.

'Can you remember your dream, Erasmo?'

'My dream?' repeated Erasmo. 'I did have an exhausting dream but I can't recall what it was about.'

'I can,' said Ulric.

They all looked at Ulric.

'You dreamt about getting me home to Dragonacres on a magic carpet.'

'A magic carpet,' shouted Palmiro, jumping into the air. 'A real magic carpet. Hooley Dooley!'

'Yes, in my dream you were riding on a magic carpet,' exclaimed Erasmo, rubbing his eyes. He looked at Ulric.

'How did you know that?' he asked.

'Something happened after you gave me that special potion. If I'm near you I can see into your dreams, and if I want to, I can also tell what you are thinking,' admitted Ulric.

'That's fantastic Uncle Ulric. Tell me what I'm thinking,' screamed Palmiro.

'One thing at a time,' said Erasmo, scratching his head. 'Ulric, can you tell me where I got this magic carpet from?' he asked.

'In your dream it belonged to a relation of Zephyrine's. It was a gold carpet with crimson fringes.'

'Is there really one, Dad?' asked Palmiro, bouncing up and down.

'Your mother's Great Aunt Teodora used to ride on a gold-coloured carpet. And I seem to recall it was full of magic.'

'Hooley Dooley!' yelled Palmiro again. 'So it's real. Can I have a go on it when we get home? You, too, Horatio.'

'Now calm down,' said Erasmo, 'I need to think for a moment.'

After a while Ulric said, 'And what you are thinking is the only answer.'

Eight

Getting Extra Help

They all knew that extra help was needed to get Ulric to Dragonacres.

If Great Aunt Teodora's magic carpet could be found, that would be the best solution. Otherwise they would have to wait until Ulric felt strong enough to fly again – which could take a long time. They discussed what they should do.

It was decided that Erasmo would stay with Ulric. Palmiro, together with Horatio, would fly home and ask Zephyrine if she knew the whereabouts of the magic carpet.

'Now you two,' said Erasmo, 'I want you to be sensible. Fly directly home. No detours. Your mother will sense when you are nearby and I imagine she will send one of your brothers to meet you. Remember to explain everything.'

'Yes,' said Palmiro.

'And I don't want you using the carpet,' added Erasmo. 'If it is found, then either Mungo or

Murgatroyd should fly back here with it, perhaps with you Horatio. Now any questions?'

'Am I allowed to fly fast with Horatio?' asked Palmiro.

'Not recklessly fast,' answered his father. 'Horatio, you will look after him, won't you?'

'Of course I will,' said the Falcon.

'If you leave now you should be home before the sun disappears,' said Erasmo, and he hugged his son. Palmiro then hugged his Uncle.

Horatio wanted to hug Ulric too, but instead flew onto his shoulder and told him that he'd be back as quickly as he could. Horatio could see a tear in Ulric's eye.

'All this for silly old me,' said Ulric, as he blinked away his tears.

At Dragonacres, Zephyrine was busy in her new kitchen. She leaned across her smooth granite work surface and pushed her muzzle out of the open window. Her nostrils twitched, the air outside was cold. Yesterday she had sensed that her beloved Erasmo and Palmiro were on their way home. Now she wasn't so sure. So that morning she'd sent word for Mungo and Murgatroyd to come home. She expected them within the hour. Returning to the cake she was making, she rinsed some pine cones under running water, dried her hands on the green polka dot apron she was wearing and reached for the cone grater. This cake recipe was a favourite of Erasmo's and she wanted to surprise him with it. It will soon be Christmas, thought Zephyrine. There was lots to do.

Where had Erasmo and Palmiro got to? Maybe they were persuading Uncle Ulric to come back with them for the holidays. Ulric would take some persuading, noted Zephyrine, as she pushed the large cake tin into her rock oven. She hummed a happy tune as she thought about Christmases years ago spent with Ulric.

'I haven't flown this fast for ages,' screamed Palmiro, as he flew alongside Horatio. 'This is really flying,' he added, as he whizzed through the air.

'Not too fast,' said Horatio, catching him up.

'Once we get Uncle Ulric on that magic carpet we'll get him flying as fast as this,' said Palmiro.

'I hope the carpet can be found,' said Horatio, 'Ulric looked sad and tired when we said goodbye.'

'He'll cheer up once we get him home,' answered Palmiro. 'Mum's cooking cheers everyone up. And see that village ahead? We'll be home soon.'

In the distance, nestling in a valley, Horatio could see a snow-covered village.

Roof-tops sparkled in the wintry sunshine.

'Look, Horatio, it's been snowing here,' shouted Palmiro gleefully. 'We live over those hills, behind this little village. Our home is called Dragonacres.'

'Dragonacres,' repeated Horatio, his thoughts quickly returning to Ulric and the whereabouts of the magic carpet.

Back in her kitchen, Zephyrine was talking to her twin sons.

'I knew your father and Palmiro were on their way home yesterday, and now I sense something has delayed them.' She paced the floor. 'It wasn't a whim. I could clearly sense that they were coming home, and now I am picking up very little.'

'Please don't worry, Mum,' said Murgatroyd, 'With it being Christmas next week Dad may have stopped off to do some shopping.'

'Shopping? Your father? I very much doubt it. No, something has happened. What I'd like you to do is fly south and see if you can sense anything. Ask whoever is around, then come straight back and we'll decide what to do next.'

'We'll go straight away,' said Mungo, and he gave

his mum a hug. Murgatroyd kissed his mum's cheek.

'I have a good feeling they are not far away,' he whispered, as they walked into the south garden.

She watched as they took to the air. They almost flew from a standing position. The muscles in their hind legs strong enough for a vertical take off.

An hour later, Horatio, with his excellent long-distance vision saw two large dragon-like shapes in the late afternoon sky.

'Palmiro, look,' he called.

Palmiro had already seen his brothers and blew a spectacular fire-breath greeting.

Horatio let Palmiro fly ahead. Palmiro's brothers seemed enormous, he thought. Although he had got used to being around large-sized dragons he was again struck by how massive they were. The three dragons made a lot of noise as they flew around each other. Palmiro beckoned to Horatio.

'Horatio,' called Palmiro, 'come and meet my twin brothers; Mungo and Murgatroyd.'

Horatio flew alongside Palmiro.

'This is my new friend, Horatio, who is Uncle Ulric's special companion,' said Palmiro, before telling his brothers of Ulric's plight.

'Good to meet you Horatio. Hop onto my back

and I'll fly you the rest of the way home,' said Murgatroyd. Palmiro climbed onto Mungo's back.

Horatio, delighted to take a rest, secured himself onto Murgatroyd's back just above his wing. As they travelled he could hear Palmiro talking quickly, telling his brothers about the need for Great Aunt Teodora's magic carpet.

Zephyrine, shielding her eyes from the low sun, watched as Mungo and Murgatroyd returned with Palmiro and the Falcon.

'Palmiro, my darling,' she cried, wrapping her arms around him tightly. 'Where is your father?'

She hadn't yet noticed Horatio, who had hopped from Murgatroyd's back and had perched himself on the top of a statue of a winged lion.

'Dad is fine. He's with Uncle Ulric, but...'

Palmiro's 'but' was interrupted by Murgatroyd. 'Mother, you haven't said hello to Horatio.'

Zephyrine spun round. Seeing the Peregrine Falcon she smiled.

'Do forgive my rudeness,' she said.

'Horatio is my new friend,' blurted Palmiro. 'He's Uncle Ulric's companion and he rescued me when I was lost.'

'Lost?' repeated his mother.

'Welcome to our home Horatio, I look forward to getting to know you,' said Zephyrine.

Horatio looked at her. She was the most beautiful dragon he had ever seen.

She was much smaller than her sons, yet strong looking. Her bright green eyes sparkled with kindness. Her lustrous scales, reflected in the afternoon sunlight, gave the impression that she wore an aura of gold. Horatio held his breath. He longed to touch her with his wing. Wanted her to greet him like she had Palmiro. He wished at that moment she was his mother, too. Spellbound by her beauty he couldn't speak.

Zephyrine bent down and put her heart-shaped face next to his.

'Do you speak, Horatio?' she asked gently.

Horatio found his voice,

'I do,' he managed to answer.

'You must be tired little one,' she said to Horatio, and she cupped her hands around his body. Horatio shivered with delight. 'Palmiro, all of you, come inside and tell me what it is that has delayed your father.'

Once settled in the warm kitchen, Palmiro told his mother everything and about Uncle Ulric being unable to fly.

Mungo and Murgatroyd immediately offered to

go to Ulric and between them carry him home.

'If it can be located, I think that magic carpet would be the best solution,' said Horatio. 'Ulric is a proud dragon and although I think it's very gracious of you both to offer to carry him, I think he would feel especially old if that were to happen.'

'I agree with you,' whispered Zephyrine. 'Ulric is old, he should be proud of his years, but he's stubborn,' she said. 'And I know he would prefer to travel here in style. He'd hate to be carried.'

'Why?' asked Mungo.

'For reasons you'll only understand when you get older darling,' she said.

'Now, locked away in my secret cupboard I do have Great Aunt Teodora's magic carpet, but it doesn't work for everyone.'

'Hooley Dooley. You have the magic carpet!' cried Palmiro, jumping up and down.

'I'll go and get it,' said Zephyrine, disappearing through one of the many open arches.

Horatio noticed how lightly she stepped from the room. He watched her delicate shadow until it, too, disappeared.

'If the carpet doesn't work, we could carry Ulric back at night time,' suggested Murgatroyd. And they then discussed the merits of night travel. Horatio discovered that Mungo and Murgatroyd could even see through banks of heavy fog.

Palmiro took a walk around the kitchen,

'That's another new thing,' he said, 'I didn't know mum had a secret cupboard.'

'You don't know everything,' said Mungo.

'Hmm,' said Palmiro, spinning round on his heels as he smelt the cake cooling by the window. Seeing the sugared cones he licked his lips.

'Did Mum bake this for me?' he asked.

'For you and father, I think,' answered Murgatroyd, 'but I suggest you have some vegetable broth before cake,' he said pointing to a huge pan simmering on the stove.'

'Vegetable broth first. Yuck,' said Palmiro turning up his nose. I will have a slice of cake, he decided, cutting himself a large chunk.

Zephyrine re-appeared carrying a rolled up carpet. It was covered in dust. She handed it to Mungo and told him to go outside and shake it gently and not to let go of it.

'So how do you make it fly, Mum?' asked Palmiro, with his mouth full of cake.

'From what I can remember,' began Zephyrine, 'Great Aunt Teodora used to sit on it and give exact directions.'

When Mungo returned they marvelled at the carpet's golden threads. Zephyrine touched the fringe of red tassels.

'Let's try it,' shouted Palmiro, abandoning his cake.

His mother put her arm out, 'No, no, no. You mustn't regard it as a play-thing. This is a carpet that demands respect. It had one owner for a very long time – you can't just try it out. It must be taken at once to your Uncle Ulric and I hope it works for him. If it doesn't I will have to get it mended.'

After further discussion Mungo and Murgatroyd and Horatio set off. Horatio was appointed as navigator and was again invited to sit on Murgatroyd's back. Mungo rolled up the carpet and carried it under his arm. Palmiro stayed behind with his mother.

It was a cold night, and a north wind was beginning to blow. Zephyrine gave them a huge flask of broth and an everlasting hot water bottle for Ulric, who, she sensed would be feeling the cold.

Ulric was shivering. His temperature had plummeted and Erasmo was becoming concerned.

'Stop worrying about me,' said Ulric, reading Erasmo's mind, 'I've just got the shivers,' he said, through chattering teeth.

'Maybe we should do some exercises,' offered Erasmo, and he began to run on the spot. 'It would help you, Ulric,' he said, taking big leaps into the air.

'I haven't got any energy to jump up and down. I want to go to sleep,' said Ulric.

'But I don't think you should go to sleep,' said Erasmo, 'Let's play some games. What about walking around and playing I spy with my beady eye?'

'I spy,' repeated Ulric, 'I haven't played that for ages. I'll go first, but I'm sitting here to play it,' he said. 'I spy with my beady eye something beginning with… "S" '

'S' repeated Erasmo, 'A stream?'

'No.'

'Stones?'

'No.'

'Straw?'

'No.'

'Stars?'

'No.'

'Strangers?'

'No,' said Ulric, looking round.

'Sycamore seeds?'

'No, no!' shouted Ulric.

'Oh I give up,' said Erasmo.

'Sleep,' said Ulric, closing his eyes.

Erasmo shook him. 'You mustn't go to sleep Ulric, your temperature will drop even further.'

Ulric opened his eyes.

'I'm very, very cold,' he said, 'My bones feel like ice.'

Erasmo looked at the small fire he had lit and built it up with more dry leaves and twigs. He began to rub Ulric's back. Once his back felt warmer he rubbed Ulric's neck.

'Too hard,' moaned Ulric, 'you'll rub my scales off.'

There's no pleasing you, thought Erasmo, continuing to rub hard. He was aware that Ulric would read his thoughts, so he continued to think of things that would keep Ulric awake, if argumentative.

Nine

The Magic Carpet

Horatio was enjoying his ride on Murgatroyd's back. It was a totally different sensation to flying oneself. To keep warm Horatio wrapped his wings across his chest. He thought again about Ulric.

'Will this magic carpet work for Ulric?' he shouted into Murgatroyd's ear.

'I have a feeling it will,' answered Murgatroyd. 'Mum did say it preferred older dragons. I suppose it depends on whether or not it likes Ulric.'

It will like Ulric. It must like Ulric, thought Horatio.

As they began their descent Horatio could see Ulric and Erasmo sitting by a camp-fire and he could hear singing.

'Look, Ulric ,' cried Erasmo, breaking off from a favourite dragon song, 'our rescuers!'

Ulric and Erasmo shouted and waved. There was no need, they had been seen.

'Dad,' shouted Mungo, landing first.

Horatio flew from Murgatroyd's back and landed next to Ulric.

'My goodness,' said Ulric staring at Mungo and Murgatroyd, 'look at the pair of you. How you've grown.'

'Good to see you Uncle Ulric,' they both said.

'I've been having a little rest,' said Ulric, by way of explanation. 'My old wings have been giving me a bit of trouble.' He winked at Horatio.

Erasmo took the carpet from Murgatroyd, smoothed it out and lay it on the ground.

'Does your mother think this will work?' he asked. As they watched, the carpet curled one of its corners.

Horatio spoke first. 'Yes. Zephyrine thinks it will work perfectly for Ulric,' he said, before any doubt could set in. 'Apparently it must be given clear instructions.'

Mungo and Murgatroyd both nodded their heads in agreement.

'How fast does it travel?' asked Ulric, staring at the carpet.

No one appeared to know.

'Mum sent this too,' said Mungo, handing Ulric the everlasting hot-water bottle.

'Bless your dear mother,' said Ulric, taking the bottle and holding it close to his chest.

'And here's a flask of broth,' said Murgatroyd.

Erasmo gave a deep sigh. What with his two strong sons here, a flask of delicious vegetable broth, and Great Aunt Teodora's magic carpet, he knew all would soon be well.

They quickly shared the broth while discussing their journey. It was decided that Ulric would get airborne on the carpet first, then the others would set off behind him. Horatio, relieved to see Ulric looking better began to feel tired himself. He hoped that Murgatroyd would again invite him to travel on his back. Horatio would have loved to have flown on the carpet with Ulric but knew that there was a better chance of the carpet accepting one new occupant than two.

'You can ride on me again, little one,' said Murgatroyd, almost reading his thoughts.

'Little one,' repeated Ulric, 'is this a new name?'

Horatio didn't know what to say.

'Mum called him "little one",' said Mungo, gently stroking Horatio's back.

'Come along now, Ulric. This is the moment,' said Erasmo.

As softly as he could Ulric stepped onto the carpet. They all watched. The carpet quivered then became still.

'Dear Carpet,' said Ulric politely, 'can you please take me to Dragonacres?'

The carpet straightened itself, but remained on the ground.

'It's not moving,' cried Ulric.

'Try again,' said Erasmo.

'I say, dear Carpet, can you take me to Dragonacres?' he asked again.

The carpet rose a few inches and hovered. Ulric wobbled.

'Try sitting down,' suggested Erasmo. Ulric carefully sat down and crossed his legs.

'I think it's warming up,' said Erasmo. As he spoke the carpet returned to the ground with a thud. Ulric fell sideways.

'Ouch,' he said, 'that wasn't very nice.'

The carpet, free of Ulric rolled itself up.

'What about mentioning Great Aunt Teodora,' whispered Horatio.

Ulric cleared his throat,

'I say, dear Carpet, can you remember a lady dragon called Teodora, who you served so dutifully for many, many moons? It just so happens that a close relative of hers has, in my hour of need, sent you to me.'

The Carpet stretched out. Using its fringe it

beckoned to Ulric. Everyone held their breath as Ulric stepped on to the carpet and sat down.

'Please don't throw me about. I am old and my weary bones ache.'

Beneath him the carpet rippled.

Ulric felt like Father Christmas flying in the night sky

Ulric continued, 'Your services are now required to take me back to Dragonacres. Dragonacres and no further. I don't wish to impose.'

Ulric had found the right words. The carpet rose steadily, before moving forward at a gentle speed.

'Come along,' shouted Ulric to the others.

Horatio flew onto Murgatroyd's back. He no longer felt tired; the sight of Ulric riding up into the night sky on a magic carpet was enough to keep anyone awake.

'I could get used to this,' cried Ulric, enjoying himself. After he'd spoken the carpet flew even faster.

Mungo and Murgatroyd, with Horatio on his back, flew at either side of the carpet, Erasmo was behind them.

Horatio could tell that Ulric was happy, and he was happy too. At last they were beginning their holiday. As they journeyed along it began to snow.

'It will be Christmas soon,' shouted Ulric.

'I feel rather like Father Christmas must do flying through the night sky. All I need are a few exciting presents and I could be Santa himself.'

No sooner had he said these words when an assortment of boxed and wrapped packages landed beside him.

'Goodness me,' cried Ulric, gathering them close. He looked up. 'Where have they come from?' he asked.

Mungo and Murgatroyd shook their heads.

I'd better be very careful about what I say,' said Ulric, putting a finger to his lips. Holding on to the packages he managed the rest of the journey in silence. No one else said very much either. They were all intent on getting safely home, it had been a long day and it was almost midnight.

As they approached Dragonacres, Erasmo could see that lights had been left on for them. He could even make out Zephyrine's lovely silhouette by the window.

The dragons began their descent. The Carpet, knowing where it was heading, skilfully lowered itself to the ground. It stopped in front of the south door where Zephyrine and Palmiro were waiting.

'Ulric!' cried Zephyrine. Ulric wobbled slightly as he tried to stand up; Zephyrine reached out to steady him.

'What an amazing experience,' said Ulric, stepping from the Carpet. Horatio flew onto Ulric's shoulder, and Erasmo wrapped Zephyrine tightly in his arms.

'Goody, goody, Christmas presents,' shouted Palmiro excitedly.

'What was the ride like Uncle Ulric?' he asked.

'The best ride I've ever had,' exclaimed Ulric. Then turning to the Carpet he said, 'Thank you dear Carpet, for an exciting and enjoyable ride. I am indebted.'

Mungo and Murgatroyd collected the wrapped

packages and carried them inside. The carpet rolled itself up. Ulric heard it groan as he picked it up and carried it into the warm kitchen. Propping it against the wall, his eyes lit up at the feast Zephyrine had prepared. Steam rose from an assortment of delicious looking dishes. A large table had been set with seven places. Ulric's nostrils twitched. He suddenly felt ravenous.

Sitting around the table there was much chatter. Finally, Zephyrine spoke about her dear Great Aunt Teodora. Although she couldn't remember how she had acquired the magic carpet, she did recall stories that her mother had told her about Great Aunt Teodora. She had travelled many times to Europe on the carpet, visiting relatives in the Dolomites and the Alps, before coming home with exotic treats.

'When she, Great Aunt Teodora, came home she'd always take a nap,' said Zephyrine. 'One of her naps lasted for almost a year. Whenever she woke the carpet would be ready to take her to wherever she wished to go. She barely flew in those days. She did say that at her age, it was more dignified to travel by carpet.'

'Maybe the carpet will decide to adopt you, Ulric,' said Erasmo.

'That would be simply marvellous,' said Ulric.

'Two old relics flying together,' he added, and they all laughed.

'Look at the time,' said Erasmo, yawning. 'We all need a long rest. Not a nap of the duration Great Aunt Teodora would take, we don't want to miss Christmas.'

Palmiro was already asleep with his head on the table, but he opened his eyes at the mention of Christmas.

'Little one,' said Zephyrine, looking at Horatio, 'I know that Palmiro wants you to sleep in his room, so come with me.' She held out her arm for Horatio, 'I've prepared you a small bed, by an open window. I hope you like it. And Ulric, I've prepared your bed in the west wing, in the heated, master bedroom.'

'My dear Erasmo and Zephyrine,' said Ulric, standing up, 'I am… we are,' he said, looking at Horatio, 'delighted to be here with you all. And I can tell this is going to be a very special holiday indeed.'

Ten

Almost Christmas Eve

Ulric was at last feeling like his old self. Stretched out on the heated marble bed, he couldn't remember a December morning when he'd felt so warm and comfortable. He turned over and sighed. Five minutes later the aroma of charcoaled mushrooms made his nostrils twitch. This is heaven, Ulric said to himself, opening his eyes. Instinctively he looked round for Horatio, before remembering that Horatio was sleeping in Palmiro's room. Palmiro had been having nightmares and had asked Horatio to stay with him. Ulric missed his feathered friend, but understood Palmiro's need for a night-time companion. I must talk to Palmiro today about getting rid of those nightmares, decided Ulric, as he got up.

The stone floor was smooth and warm under his feet. Enjoying the sensation Ulric walked to the window. He stood for a moment in front of the magic carpet that was leaning against the wall.

'Good morning Carpet,' he said, patting it, and, as he did so, he heard it groan.

'Are you speaking to me?' asked Ulric mischievously.

The Carpet shrugged but remained silent. Ulric stared at it and remembered that he'd heard loud snoring during the night. Could it have been the Carpet? Surely not, he thought, studying it.

'I don't suppose it was you who was snoring?' asked Ulric. The Carpet shuffled a few inches along the floor.

'So you are awake?' exclaimed Ulric. The Carpet appeared to sigh.

It was Zephyrine who had suggested that the carpet stay in Ulric's room, in order for them to get used to each other. At the window Ulric pushed aside a square of rock and looked out. The day was dull and grey, the sun nowhere to be seen, but there was noise and activity. Ulric could see both Erasmo and Mungo frantically digging in the west garden. Whatever are they digging for, he wondered.

After splashing his face with warm water Ulric hurried along to the kitchen.

'Good morning everyone,' he shouted.

'Good morning, Ulric,' responded Zephyrine, and she stood on her tip-toes to kiss his cheek.

Palmiro was already seated at the table. He was holding his head in his hands.

'Uncle Ulric, last night I had another scary dream,' he wailed. 'Horatio heard me.'

'You didn't have scary dreams when you stayed with me,' said Ulric.

'I know,' said Palmiro. 'Why do I have them now?'

'I don't know,' said Ulric, 'but today we'll find out,' he said reassuringly.

'I think,' said Zephyrine, who was dishing up breakfast, 'that you eat sweet things too late, and somehow it brings on bad dreams.'

'That may, in part, be true,' agreed Ulric, spearing a huge mushroom with his fork.

'Now, Palmiro, tell me about these scary dreams of yours?'

'There is a monster, but I only half see him,' said Palmiro. 'I know it is waiting for me; hiding behind some bushes. Then it gets dark and I have to walk across a frozen lake to get home. It is so frightening because I know if I don't wake myself up I will fall through the ice or the monster will get me.' Palmiro rubbed his eyes.

Zephyrine walked over to her son and cradled his head in her arms.

'That is a very bad dream,' agreed Ulric. 'Much

of which is to do with the shock of falling into that frozen lake.'

Zephyrine stroked her son's head, 'My poor darling,' she cooed.

'So how can I stop these dreams Uncle?'

'Let me think about it,' said Ulric, chewing. 'I will find the answer.'

'Every night I'm scared of going to sleep,' said Palmiro.

'You mustn't think like that. Today we will plan how to destroy that dream monster,' said Ulric, reaching for another mushroom.

Horatio flew into the room.

'Hello little one, would you like some mushrooms?' asked Zephyrine, who hadn't quite got used to what Horatio liked to eat.

'No, thank you,' said Horatio, staring at the giant mushrooms, 'I ate my breakfast earlier.'

Horatio settled himself on the back of Ulric's chair.

'I need to talk to you later about Palmiro's bad dreams,' whispered Ulric. Horatio nodded his head.

'Look at the size of these,' shouted Mungo, entering the kitchen with his father.

They were both carrying two enormous root vegetables.

'Are they what I think there are?' asked Ulric.

'They are,' answered Zephyrine, 'I'm going to roast those Jumberlines as a special treat for our Christmas feast.'

'Purple Jumberlines,' cried Ulric, 'I haven't tasted roasted Jumberline for almost a hundred years,' he said, as he helped himself to the last mushroom.

After breakfast, Ulric took a walk around the grounds of Dragonacres. He wanted to be on his own to think how to help Palmiro. The air was cold and refreshing. He marvelled at Erasmo's good fortune. Not only had he married the beautiful Zephyrine, but he lived at Dragonacres. A majestic home if ever there was one. Of course it had been passed down from generation to generation, but Erasmo had worked hard to extend both the living accommodation and the gardens, and in the process added many creature comforts. Ulric rubbed his emerald ring, I must talk to Palmiro about the power of semi-precious stones, he thought, heading towards the south garden.

Palmiro and Horatio were having a conversation by the ornate pond. Horatio was perched on the top of a large stone fish which acted as the fountain's spout. Long icicles hung from the fish's open mouth.

'Horatio,' do you remember me falling through the ice into that lake?' asked Palmiro.

'I do. I felt so helpless,' answered Horatio.

'In my bad dreams, I have to walk across ice because there is a big monster behind me.'

Horatio remembers Palmiro falling into the icy lake

'That is a terrible dream,' said Horatio.

'It is,' agreed Ulric, catching up with them.

Horatio flew from the fountain and landed on Ulric's arm.

'Today we are going to banish these bad dreams,' said Ulric. 'First I need to fetch something from my room.'

Returning to his room Ulric was surprised to see the magic carpet having a rest on his bed.

'Ah there you are,' said Ulric, as though this were nothing out of the ordinary. The Carpet waved it's fringe at him before turning over. Ulric, having other things on his mind, ignored the Carpet and took from his bag a small piece of rose quartz. This will help Palmiro, he whispered to himself. Closing his bedroom door quietly behind him, he headed back to Palmiro.

'We were just saying,' said Horatio, 'perhaps you should sleep with Palmiro then you would be able to see into his dreams and stop them.'

'I could do that of course, but it wouldn't be a long-term solution. You see each of us is the keeper of our dreams. So it would be better for Palmiro to learn to be not only the keeper but also the master of his dreams. I have some things that will help,' said Ulric, and he passed Palmiro the rose quartz crystal.

Palmiro took it from him.

'You must place that underneath your pillow,' said Ulric. You've had a shock. Falling into that frozen lake was enough to give any dragon bad dreams. The rose quartz is a gentle stone. It promotes love, friendship and peace and will help to protect you from nightmares and night fears. As for that monster we need to draw some funny faces.'

'Funny faces?' asked Palmiro, staring into the rose quartz crystal.

Ulric nodded. Horatio had seen Ulric draw before. One winter, before they'd had a proper fire, he'd decorated their cave with a drawing of a huge fire to keep them warm. And it had worked. But how would drawing funny faces help Palmiro with his bad dreams, wondered Horatio.

In the sand garden Ulric began to draw a silly face. It was a face made up of many shapes, each with three long noses.

Palmiro began to laugh. 'Uncle, that is truly silly,' he said.

'You draw one,' said Ulric.

Palmiro knelt in the sand and drew a round, smiley face, with three eyes surrounded by seven hairy ears.

'Very good,' said Ulric. 'Now tell me, in your dream what kind of face does this monster have?'

Palmiro stopped laughing.

'His face is long and pointed with a lot of teeth. He is truly scary.'

'We can change that,' said Ulric. 'What about making these faces into silly masks. Then in your dream when you know you are going to see this monster you can make him wear a silly mask.'

'How can I do that?' asked Palmiro.

'It is your dream. You control it. All you have to

'Draw a funny face in the sand,' said Ulric

do is say, "Hey buddy, this is my dream, my rules. So wear this,' answered Ulric.

'Will that work?' asked Palmiro, a smile spreading across his face, 'because if it does this will be the best idea you have ever ever had,' he said, throwing his arms around his uncle's neck.

After lunch, charcoal and cardboard were found and soon Palmiro was busy at the kitchen table making masks.

'I think I'll have a little rest,' said Ulric, patting his tummy, which was full of two helpings of snail and gorse pie.

Approaching his bedroom door, Ulric wondered where he would find the Carpet. He hoped that it wouldn't be on his bed as he wanted to stretch out and have a snooze.

Opening the door quietly he peered inside. The Carpet wasn't on the bed, nor was it leaning against the wall. Ulric looked at the window he had left open and for an awful moment thought the Carpet had flown away.

Then he saw it. It was lying across the ceiling. Ulric was relieved that the Carpet hadn't gone anywhere.

'Are you alright up there?' Ulric called out.

To his astonishment the Carpet fluttered down. Landing on the floor it said, 'I am, thank you very much.'

'So you do have a voice. And it is sweet and magical sounding,' said Ulric.

'That is because I am magical,' replied the Carpet. 'Would you like to take another ride?' it asked.

'Well, I was going to have a rest, but, if you are suggesting a ride, then why not,' answered Ulric, 'Shall I carry you outside?'

'There's no need,' answered the Carpet. 'Alight and I will squeeze us both through the window.'

'I'm far too wide to get through that window,' exclaimed Ulric.

'Trust me,' said the Carpet, 'I'm magical, remember.'

Ulric did as he was told. He sat on the Carpet and pulled his legs close to his chest. The Carpet rose a few feet and headed towards the small window. Ulric closed his eyes and tried to make himself as small as possible. He waited to be hurled against the wall, but the next thing he felt was cold air chilling him. Opening his eyes he could see Dragonacres a hundred feet below them. As he shivered a fine cashmere blanket appeared. This he wrapped around his body and he was soon as warm as toast.

'Where are we going?' he asked.

'To get some more Christmas presents,' answered the Carpet.

When Palmiro had finished making masks he couldn't decide which one was the silliest.

'I'll ask Uncle Ulric,' he cried.

'Palmiro, leave him. He has gone for a rest,' said Zephyrine.

Horatio knew that Ulric wasn't resting; he'd seen him riding away from Dragonacres.

'So where exactly are we going?' asked Ulric. 'We mustn't go too far,' he said, aware that the others didn't know he'd gone out.

'I am taking you to a Christmas market, where you can only go if invited,' said the Carpet, beginning its descent.

Ulric could see masses of brightly coloured market stalls and many dragons busy shopping.

'There are two stalls we must visit. They both have a parcel waiting for us,' said the Carpet. 'Carry me and I will show you where to go.'

Ulric again did as he was told. It had been a long time since he'd done any shopping and he had forgotten what fun it was. At the corner of the market there was a middle-aged dragon roasting chestnuts on an open fire.

'I must have some of these,' said Ulric, patting his tummy.

With a bag of hot chestnuts in one hand and the carpet rolled up under his arm, he approached the first stall.

'Are you Ulric?' asked a young female dragon.

'I am,' he replied.

'Then this is for you,' she said, handing him a small box wrapped in pretty paper.

'What fun,' said Ulric, taking the package from her and moving to the next stall.

'Look at these,' he exclaimed, as he approached a stall full of party masks.

'I must take this one for Palmiro,' he said, picking up a yellow smiley mask with masses of orange hair attached.

'This way now,' said the Carpet, directing Ulric to where a larger package was waiting for them.

'Who are these presents from?' asked Ulric, tucking the large parcel under his free arm, before stopping at a stall selling candy-floss.

'They are from Zephyrine's Great Aunt Teodora. She left instructions for me to hand over the Christmas presents for whoever was staying with Zephyrine, once I was flying again. Four arrived the night I brought you to Dragonacres, and these two make six.'

'Who are they for?' asked Ulric, who thought they needed seven.

'For Zephyrine, Palmiro, Erasmo, Mungo, Murgatroyd and yourself.'

'What about Horatio?' asked Ulric, 'We can't leave him out.'

'What would he like?' asked the Carpet.

'I don't know, I've never had to find him a present before.'

'Well, look into his heart and see if you can find the answer,' said the Carpet.

'I'll do that,' said Ulric, 'I'll do that tonight.'

It was dark as they rode back. Seeing the lights of Dragonacres, Ulric remembered to close his eyes as they approached his bedroom window. The carpet flew into his room and gently fluttered down onto Ulric's bed.

'A perfect landing,' said Ulric, jumping up.

'My landings are always perfect,' replied the carpet, shaking itself.

To Ulric's surprise Horatio was perched on the back of his dressing table.

'Are you having fun?' asked Horatio.

'We are, we are,' answered Ulric, as he helped the Carpet to roll itself up.

'I've, I mean, we've, been Christmas shopping,' he said, beckoning to Horatio.

Horatio looked directly at Ulric. 'I have something I want to ask you,' he said.

'Ask away,' said Ulric, sitting down on his bed.

'Years ago, you rescued me from that fire in the north. Well, now we are in the north I have been wondering if I have any relatives nearby. I am very happy with you Ulric, but seeing you with your family has made me wonder about mine.'

Ulric cupped his hands around Horatio.

'You are feeling homesick,' said Ulric, 'how selfish of me not to have noticed.'

'I'm not homesick, but I have thought a lot about my mother. I wonder if I should try to find her. Can you remember exactly where you found me all those years ago?'

'I think I can,' said Ulric, scratching his head.

'I will stay at Dragonacres until Palmiro gets rid of his bad dreams,' said Horatio. 'I wouldn't want to leave him sleeping alone just yet. Then I will try and find my mother.'

Ulric looked at his dearest friend. Had the Carpet heard Horatio's wish? The Carpet shook its fringe – the message had been received loud and clear.

Eleven

Christmas Day

On Christmas morning Palmiro was too excited to open his present. He stood in the middle of the kitchen, telling everyone how he'd shouted at the monster in his nightmare.

'I sorted him, Uncle Ulric,' he bellowed, 'I told him like you said I should. I said: " Hey buddy, this is my dream. I'm in control here. You have to wear one of my silly masks." And guess what happened? He got smaller and smaller, and then the monster ran away.'

'Well done,' said Ulric, clapping his hands.

Palmiro thumped the air with his fist. 'It felt so good shouting at him,' he said, 'and watching him getting smaller and smaller. He's gone now, but I'll be ready for him if he comes back.' Palmiro skipped across the kitchen floor.

'He won't come back,' said Ulric, adding 'we should all confront our monsters. They make us miserable otherwise.'

'We can't be miserable on Christmas Day,' said Erasmo.

'No we can't,' agreed Ulric, 'Let's open our presents. I have one for each of us, mysteriously arranged by Great Aunt Teodora and delivered via the magic carpet.'

'Yippee! Presents,' shouted Palmiro, cart-wheeling to the table.

Horatio flew into the west garden. He didn't expect a present and wanted to stretch his wings. He was free now. Palmiro had learnt how to banish his bad dreams, and Ulric was happy among his relatives. Maybe it is time for me to move on, thought Horatio. He felt sad at this thought. Most of his life had been spent with Ulric, and it had been a happy time. He knew if he left, Ulric would be sad too.

Thoughts of finding his own mother occupied his mind. He longed to find out where she lived. Horatio wondered if he should talk to Ulric again. He'd grown to respect Ulric's wisdom, but Ulric wouldn't want him to leave today, or tomorrow. It would be difficult.

The purple Jumberlines had been coated with herbs and were roasting in the rock oven. Their spicy aroma made Ulric's mouth water. Purple steam escaped from the oven's vent. There was much happy chatter as the dragons gathered together.

The presents from Great Aunt Teodora were stacked in the cavernous hall, under the Christmas tree. Ulric walked towards them and reached for the smallest package.

'My dear Zephyrine, you must open yours first,' he said, waving his arm with a flourish before handing it to her.

Zephyrine was looking as lovely as ever, thought Horatio, as he flew back to them.

Perhaps he should speak to her about his feelings, he thought, as she took the present from Ulric. Carefully she undid the holly-patterned paper to reveal a gold-coloured box. Opening it, she gasped before lifting out a sparkling ruby and peridot necklace. She held it against her neck. Erasmo fastened it for her.

'How beautiful,' said Zephyrine, admiring its reflection in the looking glass.'

'No more beautiful than you deserve,' whispered Erasmo, kissing her cheek.

It was an exquisite piece of jewellery. Small rubies set around seven large crystals of olive-green peridot, linked together by a gold chain.

'Me next,' shouted Palmiro, eager to know what his present was.

Ulric handed him a small package.

'Is this for me?' asked Palmiro, who was thinking one of the larger packages would have his name on it.

'This is clearly yours,' said Ulric. 'Of course I have no idea what is inside.'

Palmiro tore at the silver wrapping paper, letting it drop to the floor. 'Hooley Dooley!' he called out excitedly, as he opened the box.

'Whatever is it?' asked Zephyrine, staring at the metallic disc he was holding.

'It is the latest Moonsternav disc,' he answered, securing it to his wrist.

'Look everyone. This is the best.'

'A navigation system controlled by the moon and the stars, I believe,' said Ulric.

'Well, that's amazing. It should certainly stop you getting lost again,' exclaimed Erasmo, hopefully.

'It's fantastic, Dad,' said Palmiro. 'I shall keep it for ever and ever.'

And he held it up to show Horatio. Horatio flew to him and stared at its blue flashing light.

'You're next,' said Ulric, handing Erasmo one of the larger packages.

Erasmo studied it. 'What can this be?' he said, placing it in front of him before undoing the sparkling paper.

He, too, opened his present very carefully, as Zephyrine had done.

Taking a light-weight back-pack from a box, Erasmo declared, 'A new travel-bag. Exactly what I need. Look it's full of secret pockets.'

The travel-bag was long with two narrow portions. Ideally suited to fit a dragon's back.

'This is perfect for weekends away, Zephyrine,' he said. 'There is lots of room. I will be able to get everything we need into this.'

Three presents remained. Two heavy ones of equal size and a smaller one.

'Come on Ulric,' said Erasmo, 'What have you got?'

'I'll go last, said Ulric, passing Mungo and Murgatroyd the large packages.

The twins ripped the crimson paper from their presents to discover they had been given two volumes each on the origins of dragon lore.

'Wow,' they said in unison. 'These are a set of first editions,' said Mungo.

These were the most sought after books dragons of their age could wish for. The pages contained a

The magic carpet had turned itself into a leaf.

series of holograms. As Murgatroyd opened the first volume a single-beam reflective hologram jumped from the page. The hologram began to bubble, displaying a variety of colours before settling into a portrait of Great Aunt Teodora.

'Look everyone, it's Great Aunt Teodora,' shouted Murgatroyd. They all looked and she smiled at them.

'I am going to enjoy this book,' said Murgatroyd, staring at the smiling image.

'Before I open my present,' said Ulric, 'I need to go and check on something. I won't be long,' he said, hurrying to his bedroom.

Ulric knew before he opened his door that the Carpet had returned.

'I knew you'd be back,' said Ulric, smiling.

The Carpet was resting on his bed.

'I must say it is quite exhausting flying alone,' said the Carpet, 'And I never do, unless I have a purpose.'

'So what did you find out?' asked Ulric, eager to know.

'I travelled north until I came to the castle you had mentioned. Further north from there I came across two Peregrine Falcons. I landed nearby but they soon became suspicious of me. Knowing I'd have to follow one of them I quickly turned myself into a leaf.'

'A leaf,' repeated Ulric.

'Yes, a leaf,' said the Carpet, 'I was then able to fly behind a fast-moving falcon for quite some distance. She was quite a size, larger than Horatio. Finally, she flew to some rocky crags and rested.'

'Go on, go on,' urged Ulric, who had sat himself on the edge of his bed.

'It wasn't long before another falcon appeared, a male. They were making plans to visit their mother. I followed them, it wasn't far. When I saw their mother, I knew that I'd found Horatio's mother.'

'You've found her. Oh, well done,' said Ulric, jumping up.

'I must go and tell Horatio at once.' Ulric stood in front of his door for a second. 'You are certain it is his mother?' he asked.

'Of course I'm certain,' answered the Carpet, with some indignation.

'Then I'll push my fear to one side and…' Ulric was unable to finish what he was saying. He felt tears prick the back of his eyes.

'What is your fear?' asked the Carpet.

'My fear is selfish,' said Ulric, wiping a stray tear from his cheek. He sniffed. 'My fear is that Horatio may choose to go and live with his family.' He sniffed again. 'It would be quite natural of course. But my heart will be as heavy as the heaviest rock, if he decides to leave.'

The Carpet didn't know what to say.

Composing himself Ulric returned to the others.

'Come along, Ulric,' said Erasmo, 'you are the only one who hasn't opened his present.'

'In a moment I will,' replied Ulric. 'I need to find Horatio.' Horatio was nowhere to be seen.

'Open your present Uncle Ulric,' urged Palmiro, 'Horatio has gone out.'

Ulric took the package and tore off the festive wrapping. His mind was elsewhere. No present is going to cheer me, he thought, when I may be about to lose the most precious friend a dragon could ever have. Ulric's present was a book. A book featuring a little girl whose heart was full of dragon love. The picture on the front cover reminded Ulric of the little girl he'd seen at Appleton station that day. Not paying much attention, he left the book on the table and went to ask Zephyrine if she knew where Horatio had gone.

Zephyrine was in the kitchen setting the table for their Christmas feast. Her new necklace sparkled in the sunlight.

'Zephyrine,' called Ulric, 'do you know where Horatio is?'

'I do,' she answered, 'but he asked me not to tell.'

'Whatever do you mean,' said Ulric, looking through the window at the deep snow.

Zephyrine stopped what she was doing and turned to Ulric. She put her hand on his arm.

'Your young friend is of the age where he wants to know about his roots. He needs to understand where he came from. Things you, nor I, can tell him,' she said softly. 'He has gone to search for his family.'

'Oh no,' said Ulric, conscious of a lump in his throat.

'He did say he'd come back and tell us whatever he finds out,' said Zephyrine, taking hold of Ulric's hand.

For the first time in a long time Ulric had no appetite. Succulent slices of roast Jumberline and toasted mistletoe sat untouched on his plate. Silently he sat with his head in his hands, the twinkle gone from his eye.

'My heart feels heavy,' he sighed, 'too heavy. I need to lie down.' Leaving the table, Zephyrine followed him.

'Let me make you a drink, to ease your fears,' she

said, taking Ulric into a side room. 'Ulric, you mustn't be sad. Whatever happens you don't have to be on your own. You know you can live with us,' said Zephyrine, handing him a drink made from herbs. Ulric sipped from a pewter goblet. He felt weary. He had forgotten the deep pain that sadness brought.

'Thank you dear Zephyrine. I know I'm being a silly old fool. But I do love my feathered friend.'

'And he loves you too,' answered Zephyrine. She walked him to his bedroom door.

The Carpet was lying across Ulric's bed and was snoring lightly. Wide awake, Ulric lay next to it and wondered what he should do.

Horatio was travelling at great speed, heading north. He had eased his burdened heart talking to Zephyrine. He hoped if he found his mother, she would possess all the kind, nurturing qualities Zephyrine had. He tried not to think about Ulric, but it was hard. One moment he couldn't envisage his life without Ulric, and the next he pictured himself living among falcons.

He flew low over snow-covered moorland, and kept looking for familiar landmarks. His memory of the area was hazy. The last time he'd covered this territory was years ago with Ulric – the day after the fire.

Ahead he could see the castle on the hillside. Horatio's heart began to beat faster. This was the place, as a fledgling he'd been captured and locked in a cage.

Back at Dragonacres, Palmiro and his brothers were building a snow-dragon in the west garden. They had used lots of holly berries for the dragon's eyes and some long pieces of charcoal for its nostrils. Now it was finished.

'It looks like you, Palmiro,' teased Mungo.

'It doesn't,' said Palmiro, throwing a snowball at his brother's tail.

Mungo and Murgatroyd were quicker at making snowballs, and their aim was better. After five minutes Palmiro raised his hands and admitted defeat. Shaking snow from his body, he announced that he was going inside to play with his Moonsternav disc.

'I wish Horatio was here,' he whispered, 'we could test it out together.'

'Where's Uncle Ulric?' he asked. 'Isn't he well?'

Zephyrine, noticing the time, shook her head. Ulric was still in his room.

'I think all the excitement of riding on the carpet, and Christmas has tired him out,' she said, glancing at Erasmo.

Not for a moment did she want Palmiro to think that Horatio may be leaving. So far he hadn't noticed because he was too interested in his new navigation system.

'I bet Uncle Ulric gets up for supper,' said Palmiro. 'Shall I go and see him.'

'No, I'll go,' said Zephyrine.

She went into the kitchen and prepared a warm drink. Placing it on a tray with some berry biscuits and a candle she carried it to Ulric's room.

Knocking gently on the door she called, 'Ulric, are you awake?'

Hearing him groan, she asked, 'May I come in?'

Ulric was lying on his bed. He rubbed his red eyes.

'Have I missed Christmas?' he asked. Then, remembering his sadness, he sat up. 'Has Horatio returned?' he asked.

Zephyrine placed the tray on the dressing table and sat herself next to Ulric.

'No. Horatio isn't back yet. And I wouldn't expect him to be,' she added, fingering her new necklace. Ulric fell back on his bed.

'Now come on, what about eating something,' she said, pointing to the tray.

'I'm not hungry.'

'It doesn't matter,' she said, taking a flannel and wiping his brow.

'Oh Zephyrine, you do look after me,' he said, sitting up again.

The Carpet, now in the corner of the room, was watching them.

'I suppose I should get up, otherwise I won't sleep tonight.'

'Only do what you want to do, Ulric. And if you don't join us I'll look in again before bedtime.' Kissing the top of his head, she left him with his thoughts.

'She is the image of her Great Aunt, as a much younger dragon,' said the Carpet, 'and she exudes the same kindness too.'

Ulric nodded his head, then he whispered, 'Horatio has gone.'

'Gone,' repeated the Carpet, 'already?'

'He'd gone before I got the chance to tell him you'd found his mother,' said Ulric.

'Why didn't you wake me?' asked the Carpet.

'I didn't know what to do,' said Ulric.

'Shall we go and find him?' asked the Carpet.

'I don't know,' sighed Ulric, 'I don't want him to think I'm interfering.'

'Hmmm, a difficult decision,' agreed the Carpet.

Twelve

Horatio's Decision

Horatio flew high above the castle. He wanted to leave the area as quickly as he could but didn't know which direction to take. He circled for a moment. The moon hid herself behind a cloud. Shrouded in darkness Horatio looked down and saw lights shining from the castle's tower. Snow had made the night eerily quiet. Turning his head he half expected to see the comforting shape of Ulric or Palmiro. I wish they were with me, he thought, feeling the unfamiliar sensation of loneliness for the first time. On he flew, north over vast moorlands, not sure of where he was heading.

Ulric sat bolt upright. A tremendous thought had just entered his head.

'I have the answer,' he said to the Carpet, before rushing from his room.

Palmiro was sitting at the table, playing with his Moonsternav disc.

'Ah Palmiro,' said Ulric, sitting next to him.

'Uncle Ulric, where have you been?' asked Palmiro, pleased to have his uncle's company.

'I've been resting,' said Ulric, winking at Zephyrine.

'I couldn't find Horatio either,' said Palmiro. 'I wanted to try out my Moonsternav system with him.'

'Well,' said Ulric, 'we can try it out. Why don't we start by finding out where Horatio is.'

'Can it do that?' asked Palmiro.

'It has an advanced radar-type device,' said Ulric, taking holding of the small disc.

'Hooley Dooley!' yelled Palmiro, eager to see his Moonsternav in action.

Ulric spent a moment looking at the controls. By pressing two dials he powered the disc, the screen turned from blue to bright red.

'What now?' asked Palmiro.

'Press this and ask for the whereabouts of Horatio.'

'Can it speak?' asked Palmiro, looking from his Moonsternav to his uncle.

'No, but it will show you where he is.'

As Palmiro asked for the whereabouts of Horatio, he and Ulric stared at the disc. The red screen darkened. The disc made a clicking sound and a map appeared. A single dot of light crossed the map and stopped.

Ulric took hold of the disc. 'He can't be there,' he said, standing up. 'That is where the castle is. The castle where I found him all those years ago.'

'Wait a minute,' shouted Palmiro.

The dot of light was moving again, moving in a southerly direction.

'Look he's flying fast,' yelled Palmiro, watching the light.

'So he is,' answered Ulric, studying the screen, 'and it looks as though he is heading this way.'

Ulric pressed another control on Palmiro's Moonsternav. Some numbers appeared.

'If he continues travelling at his current speed he will arrive here before bedtime,' announced Ulric, smiling.

'Before whose bedtime?' asked Palmiro, aware that he would shortly be told to go to bed.

'Before my bedtime,' answered Ulric, patting him on the head.

Feeling better than he had all day, Ulric's tummy began to rumble. Everyone else heard it too.

'Ulric, you should eat something,' said Erasmo. Zephyrine led Ulric into the kitchen and made him a plateful of roast Jumberline sandwiches. Conscious of his empty tummy he ate the sandwiches extra quickly, and burped.

'Pardon me,' he said, putting a hand over his mouth. With much less speed he ate the crunchy tree-bark pudding, enjoying every mouthful.

When the little wooden dragon came out of the clock and announced it was Palmiro's bedtime, Palmiro was told to go to bed.

'I'll be up extra early,' he promised his uncle. 'So we can track other things with my Moonsternav,' he said, securing the disc to his wrist.

Horatio was feeling foolish. After flying beyond the castle he didn't know which direction to take. Nor had he seen any other birds. He was tired and wanted to get back to Dragonacres. He hoped everyone would in bed so he could fly in quietly and not have to explain his absence to Ulric until the morning.

It was well past midnight when Ulric said goodnight to Zephyrine and Erasmo. Zephyrine squeezed his hand and told him not to worry.

Once inside his bedroom Ulric opened the window. Cold air rushed in. The Carpet, which was again sleeping on the ceiling, shivered and turned over. Ulric lay on his bed and wondered if Horatio had found his mother. He pulled a cover up to his chin and, despite his best intentions, began to snore. He was in a deep sleep when Horatio flew quietly through his window. Hearing Horatio the Carpet fluttered down and began to flap about. Ulric woke up.

'Sorry to have woken you,' whispered Horatio.

Ulric sat up. 'Horatio,' he called, 'You've come back. Oh I've missed you,' he said, scrambling out from under his bed cover to greet Horatio.

'Did you find your family?' he asked.

Horatio, lowered his head and said, 'No. After flying over the castle I couldn't decide where to go.'

Ulric beckoned Horatio who flew onto his outstretched arm.

'We've something important to tell you, Horatio,' he said, looking at the Carpet which moved closer and leant against the bed. Ulric told Horatio how the Carpet had discovered the whereabouts of his mother.

Horatio went very quiet. Then he said, 'I must go and see her.'

'Of course you must,' said Ulric, looking at his dearest friend. The Carpet began to wave both its fringes. 'The Carpet could take you,' said Ulric.

'All day I've been wondering if my mother will remember me,' said Horatio.

'Of course she'll remember you,' said Ulric. He longed to say more but decided not to.

Horatio then said something that made Ulric's heart burst with joy.

'Ulric, will you travel some of the way with me?'

'It will be an honour,' replied Ulric.

The next morning everyone was up early. Zephyrine was sweeping the kitchen floor. Erasmo was shovelling snow from the path in the herb garden. Palmiro was playing with his Moonsternav, and Mungo and Murgatroyd were getting ready to see their girlfriends – who were also twins.

Ulric and Horatio were preparing to set off north to find Horatio's mother.

Cupping Horatio's head in her hands, Zephyrine said, 'Little one, you must listen to your heart.'

'You are part of our family now,' said Erasmo, knowing that Ulric wanted to say these words but was finding it hard. 'Whatever happens you will always be welcome at Dragonacres,' he added.

'I'm going to track your journey on my Moonsternav,' shouted Palmiro. 'Don't stay away too long Horatio because I will miss you.'

Horatio flew to Palmiro and landed on his shoulder.

'Come along, let's get going,' called Ulric, unrolling the Carpet.

Once on the ground the Carpet shook itself. Ulric, now used to this amazing mode of transport stepped onto it and sat down. Horatio flew from Palmiro's shoulder to Ulric's.

'Bye-bye,' shouted Ulric, as the Carpet took off.

The morning was bright and clear, wisps of mist hung across the valleys. Ulric and Horatio looked straight ahead. No one spoke. Once they had flown beyond the castle Ulric suggested that Horatio should fly on alone. Hearing their discussion, the Carpet made its descent about a mile from the rocky crags where Horatio's mother lived.

Ulric said he would wait for half a day and if Horatio hadn't returned he would travel back to Dragonacres. Horatio thought this was the best plan.

Working hard to hold back tears, Ulric said, 'I hope with all my heart your reunion is a joyous one. Do what you feel is right, my little friend.'

Horatio didn't know what to say. He nuzzled Ulric's neck before flying away.

It was the happiest of reunions. Horatio's mother recognised him at once and wrapped her wings tightly around him. Horatio told her everything that had happened to him and spoke endlessly about Ulric. She had never met any dragons but was grateful to Ulric for saving her young son's life. She told him about his brothers and sisters and how she'd searched for him after the fire. She also said she knew she'd see him again.

Eventually Horatio said, 'I'd like you to meet Ulric, one day.' Then he realised it had grown dark.

Ulric was back at Dragonacres. The Carpet had brought him silently home. He was wearing a brave face but Zephyrine and Erasmo could tell he was hurting inside.

'Horatio will come back soon, won't he?' asked Palmiro, who had tracked Ulric's return journey, mile by mile, on his Moonsternav.

'I hope so,' said Ulric, picking up the book he'd been given for Christmas. He'd only glanced at the cover.

Opening the book he saw that it was not only about a little girl who loved dragons but also had stories of a handsome old dragon who lived in a cave. As he turned the pages, he saw there was a picture of him in his cave.

'This is me,' he said, standing up.

Palmiro took the book from him. Turning more

Ulric turned the pages of his book and saw a picture of himself

pages, Palmiro shouted, 'Look Uncle Ulric, here is a picture of you with Horatio.'

'How extraordinary,' exclaimed Ulric, staring at it, 'this is most strange.'

'What is strange?' asked Zephyrine.

'This book has pictures of Uncle Ulric and Horatio, and little stories about them too,' said Palmiro.

'Then it must be a magic book,' said Zephyrine.

Ulric scratched his head. He'd done many things during his long life, but he'd never been in a book before. Palmiro returned to his Moonsternav and announced that he was going continued to track Horatio during the night. Ulric stared out of the window and wondered if he would ever see his best friend again.

That night as Ulric prepared for bed, he again opened his bedroom window. The Carpet was in a deep sleep and too tired to shiver. As soon as Ulric finished his warm, bed-time drink, he fell into a fitful sleep.

He dreamt of times when he was a much younger dragon, of the day he first met Zephyrine and her sister Topaz, and of introducing Zephyrine to Erasmo. Then he dreamt of the night he rescued the young and frightened Peregrine Falcon from that fire, and of how their companionship had turned into the deepest of friendships.

Ulric woke with a start. It was already dawn. Not yet ready to face the day, a day without Horatio, he pulled his cover over his head. Closing his eyes he tried to get back to sleep. Soon he heard the Carpet flapping its fringes in the way that it did when it woke. But was it the Carpet?

No, it sounded more like the flutter of wings. Ulric sat up. It was Horatio.

'My dearest, dearest friend, you're back,' said Ulric, stretching out both arms.

'I have had the most exciting time with my mother, and sisters and brothers,' said Horatio, landing next to Ulric.

'I didn't expect to see you,' said Ulric, rubbing his eyes.

'I thought you'd say that,' said Horatio.

'How is your mother?' asked Ulric.

'I found her to be gentle and strong, a bit like Zephyrine. When I told her about you she said that true friendship is one of the most important things in life.'

'She is right,' said Ulric, getting out of his bed.

'I'd like you to meet her one day,' said Horatio.

Unable to contain himself any longer, Ulric asked,

'Have you decided what you are going to do?'

Horatio looked at Ulric.

'I want to stay here with you,' he answered, 'and visit my family as often as I can.'

'You do,' exclaimed Ulric, jumping into the air. 'Carpet, did you hear that?' shouted Ulric, picking up Horatio and carrying him from his room. The Carpet followed them.

'Listen everyone, Horatio's back and he's staying,' announced Ulric to Zephyrine, Erasmo and Palmiro.

'We knew he was back. I tracked him,' yelled Palmiro. Horatio flew to the Moonsternav and stared at the flashing disc.

'It's our destiny to be together,' said Ulric.

'Have you told him about the book you got for Christmas?' asked Zephyrine.

'No I haven't,' replied Ulric, looking for his picture book to show Horatio.

'Here it is. Look Horatio, I've been given a magical book. It is all about the many adventures you and I have had. Look, it has pictures of us both.'

Horatio flew to Ulric and landed on his arm.

Ulric looked at his dearest friend.

'But let's not read the end, just yet,' he whispered.

THE END

Turn the page for things to do...

Crossword

Across

3 Palmiro cried out when he was all alone at Oaktree Crossroads – "I am ____". (4)

5 It is dangerous on frozen ponds. (3)

7 He looked after Palmiro at Oaktree Crossroads. (3)

8 Is Ulric a young dragon? (2)

9 Ulric says, about the book he has been given for Christmas – "let's not read the ____ just yet". (3)

12 Palmiro drew a funny mask with hairy ____. (4)

13 It finally came to Ulric's rescue. (6)

15 Ulric ate too many of these seeds. (8)

16 Erasmo suggested he and Ulric play this game to keep awake. (1,3)

Down

1 What did Ulric rescue the young falcon from? (4)

2 The name of Zephyrine's Great Aunt. (7)

4 The young badger cubs played in this. (4)

6 The train station Ulric visited. (8)

10 This vegetable was in the special potion. (8)

11 Ulric was tied to the tree with this. (4)

12 Ulric's half-brother. (6)

14 Palmiro made one of these for his scary monster to wear. (4)

Word Search

D	R	A	G	O	N	S	J	H	M	P
T	R	P	R	A	B	H	Z	T	U	L
E	R	A	S	M	O	L	E	A	N	E
O	U	L	G	U	L	P	K	R	G	A
D	Q	M	H	O	R	A	T	I	O	F
O	U	I	S	A	N	C	A	V	E	N
R	A	R	C	T	F	A	L	C	O	N
A	R	O	U	L	R	I	C	E	W	T
L	T	F	E	A	T	H	E	R	L	I
E	Z	E	P	H	R	Y	I	N	E	A
J	U	M	B	E	R	L	I	N	E	S

Ulric: A Dragon's Tale - Questions

The Characters:

Who are the main characters in the story?

Can you describe them?

The Story:

What happens in the story?

Your Review:

Which parts did you like and why?

Do you have a favourite part of the book?

What did the story make you think about?

Did you learn anything from the story?

Would you recommend this book to a friend?

Why?

Who would like this book?

For more about Ulric, visit his web site:

www.dragonacres.com